ALPHA BULLY

AN ENEMIES-TO-LOVERS ROMANCE

RENEE ROSE

Published in the United States of America

Renee Rose Romance

Editor: Maggie Ryan

This book is a work of fiction. While reference might be made to actual historical events or existing locations, the names, characters, places and incidents are either the product of the author's imaginations or are used fictitiously, and any resemblance to actual persons, living or dead, business establishments, events, or locales is entirely coincidental.

This book contains descriptions of many BDSM and sexual practices, but this is a work of fiction and, as such, should not be used in any way as a guide. The author and publisher will not be responsible for any loss, harm, injury, or death resulting from use of the information contained within. In other words, don't try this at home, folks!

WANT FREE RENEE ROSE BOOKS?

Go to http://subscribepage.com/alphastemp to sign up for Renee Rose's newsletter and receive a free copy of *Theirs to Protect, Owned by the Marine, Theirs to Punish, The Alpha's Punishment, Disobedience at the Dressmaker's* and *Her Billionaire Boss.* In addition to the free stories, you will also get special pricing, exclusive previews and news of new releases.

USA TODAY BESTSELLING AUTHORS

Alpha's
TEMPTATION

A billionaire werewolf romance

RENEE ROSE & LEE SAVINO

AUTHOR'S NOTE

The idea for the Wolf Ridge High series was born when Lee Savino and I were writing *Alpha's Bane*, a second chance romance in our *Bad Boy Alphas* series. The characters in the book, Trey and Sheridan, were high school sweethearts who ended badly. I wrote the flashback scenes from their high school romance while Lee worked on their present day conflict.

As I played with the idea of this pack of high school students, all going to school together and dealing not only with the raging hormones of a teenager, but also with shifter and pack dynamics, I thought it would be fun to delve deeper.

This is the result. I hope you become as addicted as I am to the teen angst and drama! :-)

CHAPTER 1

 *ailey*

THERE'S a reason I don't drive any more. A very good reason.

But moments like these make me wish I didn't turn into a hyperventilating spaz every time I even think about getting behind the wheel. Not driving means I attend the local Wolf Ridge High instead of Cave Hills.

Cave Hills, the top-rated college prep dream school.

Cave Hills the school I should be going to.

The school I deserve to go to.

The school fifteen miles away.

Without a car, it might as well be a hundred.

And at this particular moment, no car means I'm screwed.

Because the bus just passed by my house.

I hear the *ktshh* of it stopping on my street. *Ten minutes early!* Snatching my bookbag off the sofa, I dash out my front door with my teeth unbrushed and my Mexican skull Chucks untied, but it's way too late.

"Wait!" I wave and chase after it. "Hold up!" I jog a half a block, tripping and hopping in my loose sneakers.

The driver *has* to see me even if he can't hear. The students in the bus definitely see me. They stare through the windows at me. Not laughing. Not pointing.

I'm a fish in a bowl. Mildly amusing to them, but they won't feel bad if they have to flush me down a toilet in a week. Racist fucks. You'd think in Arizona being Hispanic wouldn't get me shunned.

Dammit.

I stoop to tie my shoes and sling my backpack over my shoulder. It slides forward and whacks me in the back of the head. I huff and stand.

Next door, the dynamic brother and sister duo, Cole and Casey Muchmore climb into Cole's mostly-restored 1950s classic Ford truck. If they witnessed my early morning sprint, they're not letting on.

Their dad on the other hand sits in the window with a beer in his hand, not even trying to hide the fact he's watching me. The front window is where he always is, except when he's stomping around yelling at his kids loud enough for the entire neighborhood to hear.

Right now, I swear he's smiling. Like he just had a good laugh over watching me run after the stupid bus. What an ass. Like father, like son, I guess.

Cole is as cool as his truck and even better looking. And he definitely knows it. Revels in it. He rules Wolf Ridge High like his shit comes out rosy and he doesn't have wrong-side-of-the-track stank all over him. Like the worn out, ripped jeans he practically lives in aren't covered in grease and grime from repairing cars.

No, Cole Muchmore doesn't need nice clothes, a fancy car, or anything else money can buy. He has something seen as much more valuable. He's got the status of worshipped star quarterback. And at Wolf Ridge High, that puts him somewhere in the vicinity of a god.

I eye my last chance at getting to school on time and weigh the chance of catching a ride with them.

Unlike the rest of the kids at Wolf Ridge High, the Muchmores don't just pretend they don't see me. They throw scowls in my direction. Hateful glares, even. I met them the day I moved in—went over and introduced myself because they came out to gawk.

They barely answered, looking at me like I had two heads. Tay Swift has had friendlier interactions with Kanye than I had with the Muchmores that day.

But right now I need a lift to school. Even if I walk, I'll be late for my Spanish exam, and calling my mom is out. If she has to leave work to drive me, I'll definitely get an earful about how I need to start driving again.

Besides, she has way too much on her plate with the new job.

Forcing my social anxiety to the background, I jog down the sidewalk to the curb and flag down Cole. He slows but doesn't stop. His sister Casey, a sophomore with resting bitch-face, rolls down the window.

Cole leans across her. His dark hair is tousled, his full lips twisted in a lopsided smirk. "What's wrong, Pink, miss the bus?"

Pink.

He's referring to the streak of pale pink that cuts through the front of my dark hair of course. The nickname and my unfortunate physical reaction to Cole Muchmore's nearness throws me off for a sec. *Ride.* I need a ride.

I stand on tiptoes to see into the truck and meet Cole's eye. "Yeah, any chance I could catch a ride?" I curse myself for sounding like a timid mouse.

He shrugs his shoulders with a mock-rueful expression. "Sorry, Pink. I would offer, but there's no room."

Bullshit. There's clearly plenty of room between the two siblings, and he's just being a dick. I hear his deep chuckle as his sister rolls up her window.

My face flushes hot as they drive away, and a thick knot forms in my throat, heat burning the back of my eyes.

Don't cry. Not over this.

Save your tears for the things that matter.

Like Catrina. Like the other friends I left behind in Golden.

The pep talk doesn't work. Two hot trails make their way down my face as I take off, speed walking toward school.

I hate Wolf Ridge. I really do.

I make it to the first major intersection and check the time on my phone as I wait for the light.

Gah. I'm definitely going to be late.

"Hey!" An old Subaru wagon pulls over to the curb and the back door opens. "Did you miss the bus, too?" A scrawny girl with bleach-blonde hair punked out in all directions calls out. I've seen her on my bus and around school. She's an underclassman, so we don't have classes together, but she's familiar.

"Yeah." I tense, prepared for another insult.

"Get in. My mom will take us."

Her mom beckons impatiently. She has bleached stringy hair and the prematurely aged skin of someone who drinks and smokes too much. The car reeks of cigarettes.

Relief and gratitude still slam into me like a tidal wave as I slide in the back seat. "Thanks. I was afraid I'd be late."

"I already called the school to complain about that damn bus driver," her mom rants from the front seat. "It's bullshit. They can't just show up when they feel like it. They're supposed to stick to a schedule!"

I murmur my agreement.

"I'm Rayne." The girl turns in the seat to study me. Her blue eyes are huge in her small, heart-shaped face and her nose is pierced.

I decide instantly that I like her. "Bailey."

"I know," she says, reinforcing my impression that I'm not actually invisible at Wolf Ridge High. I'm being actively shunned.

My gut clenches.

"Thanks for stopping," I say. "Cole Muchmore outright refused to take me." I don't know why I say it. I'm not one to complain and I usually keep my thoughts to myself, but I'm getting freaking desperate for someone to talk to.

Rayne rolls her eyes. "Cole is an alpha-hole, like all the other ballers."

I let out a puff of laughter. "I can't argue with that."

Alpha-hole. It's a perfect description for him.

Well, he can go fuck himself. I won't be crying over his lack of courtesy.

Guys like him do absolutely nothing for me.

We get to school on time and climb out of the Subaru. The kids getting off the bus stop to stare at us.

"What?" I demand out loud.

I swear, you'd think I was some sort of green-skinned alien from outer space.

Rayne flips them off and grabs my elbow. "Ignore them. They all do whatever the alpha-holes say like freaking minions."

"Wait… What do the alpha-holes say?"

Rayne looks away, pink staining her pale cheeks. "Nothing. Don't worry about it. This is our school, too."

Huh.

Whatever that means. I let it drop. I don't need to alienate the only person who's willing to be nice to me.

"Thanks for stopping. And for talking to me. I've been seriously losing my mind here. I thought maybe all the kids were robots like in this old movie my mom made me watch where the men had all killed their wives and exchanged them with robot replacements."

Rayne's impish face breaks into a huge smile. She holds up her palm like she's swearing an oath. "Not a robot." She lifts her chin at all the kids streaming into the school who are craning their necks to ogle us. "They might be though."

COLE

I SLIDE into my chair in journalism a few seconds after the bell rings. Of course the human—the bitch who moved next door—already sits at her desk beside me, chit-chatting with the teacher like a suck-up. I catch a whiff of her cinnamon and honey scent as I sit and my balls tighten.

"Nerd patrol," I mutter as Mr. Brumgard walks away from her desk. I heard she's taking Advanced Placement English online, and she's using this class as an elective. Double English credits. Fucking whack-job.

She fumbles her pen—probably because I rattled her—and it clatters to the ground. My buddy Austin automatically reaches to pick it up, then catches my glare and realizes who it belongs to. He straightens without retrieving it.

Good. The king of Wolf Ridge High still rules. No one will talk to Bailey, much less help her, unless I lift my ban on it. I give it another month and she'll transfer to a school where her kind belong.

She leans into the aisle to get it, but I kick it away, forcing her to lose her balance and fall halfway out of her seat, balanced on one hand. I get a flash of bare thigh as her mini-dress rides up and a low growl rises in my throat.

What the fuck is wrong with me? I don't get hot for her kind.

Miss Perfect in those little dresses and skull Chucks. I glare in her direction, willing my attraction for her to die. Unfortunately, the way her breasts stretch the front of her polka dot mini-dress today gets me hard. Which makes me hate her even more.

Even if it weren't for the situation with our parents, I would say she doesn't belong here. She's too fucking smart. Too nerd-hot. Too self-possessed for someone getting actively shunned every day at school.

And it's somehow a thousand times worse that her brains and attitude are wrapped up in that juicy little package.

Mr. Brumgard finishes taking roll, then calls out, "Pop quiz on the reading I assigned yesterday!"

The class groans. Everyone except for Bailey, who obviously can't wait to show she did her homework. Brumgard stands and starts placing a sheet of paper face down on each desk.

My eyes roll back in my head with frustration, and I fall back against my seat back. This fucking sucks. There's no chance I'll get a passing grade, and the homecoming game is Friday. Which means I'm gonna get benched. Which means the entire team and Coach Jamison are going to kill me.

My teammates look over at me with that sort of desperate question in their eyes. I shake my head and a collective underbreath groan ripples through the room. It's not just my teammates, it's the rest of the class, too.

Sports are huge at Wolf Ridge High. Way bigger than academics.

Even though we have to play our skills down around humans, every student wants to see us win. And I always put on a good show toying with the other team and dishing out cocky attitude on the field.

"You have seven minutes to complete the quiz over last

night's reading," Brumgard says, looking at his phone. "You may begin."

The rustle of paper fills the room as everyone flips their quizzes over. I pick up my pencil and stare at the words, not even comprehending what I'm reading.

My mind spins over the possible outcomes of this situation. They pretty much all end in me getting benched for not maintaining a C average and facing the wrath of the entire school.

But none of that compares to the shitstorm I'll catch at home when my dad hears.

Which is ironic, since the reason I haven't done homework all week is because I've been working late at Bo's uncle's garage to pay for groceries since my dad's too fucking drunk and depressed to get off his ass and find a new job.

My gaze slides over to Bailey. The girl I can't stand.

She's already three-quarters of the way through her quiz. And, most importantly, she hasn't taken the time to write her name on the top yet.

In one of my best asshole moves, I snap my hand out and grab her quiz while the teacher's back is turned. I slide my blank quiz on her desk.

Her cheeks color pink and her mouth drops open, but before she can make a sound, every student around us turns and stares her down, unified pack style.

She may be human, but our biology is similar enough that she must feel the pressure. Conform or die. This is wolf domination and pack dynamics at their best. And I'm their alpha.

Her lips snap closed. Jaw sets. Shooting a murderous

glare in my direction, she hunches over the paper and starts furiously writing the answers down.

The victory that explodes in my chest has more to do with breaking Bailey than it does with solving my grade problems. I've been dying to bring her to her knees since the moment she had the fucking *audacity* to move in next door.

I smirk as I write my name at the top of her paper and guess at the answers she left blank. Even if I get every one of them wrong, I'll pass.

Pink is an A plus student. Possibly semi-genius level. She doesn't belong at Wolf Ridge any more than her mom belongs at the brewery.

Anyway, the point is, her answers will be right. And all I need is a C.

I watch her finish her quiz—the one that used to be mine—brows furrowed, lips locked in a tight line.

"Time," Mr. Brumgard calls. "Pencils down. Pass your quizzes up, please."

She sends me another furious glare before passing hers up, and I flick my brows in challenge, daring her to do something about it.

She won't, and we both know it.

Score one for the alpha bully.

Loser human: zero.

CHAPTER 2

 *ailey*

FURY BURNS MY THROAT, blinds me as I stumble out of journalism class.

The *nerve* of Cole Muchmore. He literally just stole my quiz in front of the whole class and got away with it. He's fist-bumping his teammates—the other alpha-holes, as Rayne called them.

As if making me a social pariah wasn't enough, now he's stealing my work?

I can't believe I *let* him get away with it.

What's wrong with me? Am I so desperate for friends I would sacrifice my education and future just to not piss anyone off? I should have ratted him out. They already hate me. I've been a social outcast, party of one for weeks now.

And what in the hell is wrong with all the kids in this

school that they think helping the football star cheat is the right thing to do?

Assholes.

I duck my head to hide the tears blurring my vision as I spin my locker combination around. It takes me five spins before I calm down enough to even see the numbers. Three more tries to get it unlocked.

The second the door swings open, it slams shut, a big hand slapping it closed and staying there.

Of course I know exactly who that hand belongs to.

"Thanks for the help, Pink." Cole crowds against my backside, leaning in close to speak low in my ear, like this is some private, lover's conversation and not more bullying from the biggest dick in the school.

His voice rumbles deep, reverberating right into secret places it doesn't belong.

"Fuck you, Cole," I snap. I don't usually curse, especially not at school, but this situation really calls for it.

I guess I'm still a chicken, though, because I don't turn around, not willing to come eye to eye with my tormentor. I press myself even closer to the lockers to keep him from rubbing against me, but he just moves in tighter, and now I have smells and sensations that will haunt me along with his smirking face.

He's going for intimidation and it's working, but my body registers it as something altogether different.

Something foreign yet primitively familiar. Biological level, monkey brain shit that makes my downstairs unconscionably wet. Because no way do I find his muscle-brained posturing sexy.

It sucks that he's Jacob Elordi level hot. Tingles race

across the surface of my skin. I look down. Goosebumps. He's giving me fucking goosebumps just standing too close. I don't have to look to know my nipples are beading against my favorite polka dot skater dress. I fight the urge to cross my arms over my chest. He doesn't need to know how he affects me.

He's big. Strong. His voice is deep. His scent is cedar-wood soap and masculine goodness. And his cocky bull-shit does something squirmy to my core.

"Here." His other hand appears in front of my face. Not the one still holding my locker closed effectively caging me in, but one on the other side of my head. He's holding a piece of cinnamon Trident out to me.

"Really?" I snatch the gum and whirl around, too pissed now to avoid a face-to-face confrontation. "A stick of gum?" I hold it between our noses, cursing my hand for shaking. "Is this the going rate for taking someone's quiz for them around here?"

Cole's fiery brown gaze burns through me. I see the hatred in his eyes before he blinks and pretends he doesn't give a shit. He shifts to lean a shoulder against my locker. "Well, you know, that's all I can afford... seeing as how your mom stole my dad's job and all."

All the noise in my head quiets. My stomach drops out and I lose my breath. "What?"

"Yeah. I guess she's a real big shot, huh? Your mom? All the way from Coors Brewery in Colorado." He shrugs. "My dad couldn't compete with that."

My knees quake. Mouth opens and closes like an empty PEZ dispenser, but I can't figure out the appropriate response.

It doesn't matter. Cole's already pushed off and sauntered away, the crowd parting to allow its king to pass.

He thinks my mom took his dad's job?

That's why Cole and Casey Muchmore hate me? That's why I've been the social outcast here for the past eight weeks. Why I can smile and say "hi" to kids in the hallways, in the bathrooms, and not even a freshman will so much as give me a head nod.

I had no idea it was personal.

Understanding should bring relief, but it just brings a hollow ache to the pit of my stomach. Unless Cole and Casey Muchmore's alcoholic, waste of space dad gets another job, I'm public enemy number one.

And it's not my fault. It's not even my mom's fault.

She was hired in after Wolf Ridge Brewery had a major kerfuffle with the FDA and got shut down. And yeah, my mom said things were a total mess when she got here. Like the checks weren't in place to prevent contamination disasters. That means Cole and Casey's dad sucked at his job, and it's no wonder he lost it.

I can see why us moving in next door would be like rubbing salt in a wound, but my mom didn't steal his dad's job. And even if she did, how in his twisted, Neanderthal brain am I to blame for his life turning shitty?

I know quite a bit about life suddenly turning shitty. You don't see me screwing over strangers in revenge.

Fingers shaking, I work the combination on my locker once again and pull out my backpack and head to lunch, my most dreaded period of the day. The time when I try to find a place alone to sit and do my homework as I eat a sandwich.

"So you took the alpha-hole's quiz for him, huh?"

I whirl to find Rayne, standing there. Her friendly face is such a balm to my raw emotions, I want to throw my arms around her and squeeze. I hold back though. I don't want to scare my only friend off with my desperation for human contact.

"News travels that fast?"

"Yep. That's Wolf Ridge for you. Takes about five minutes for the latest news to go around. Especially when it concerns our star quarterback."

"Is football that big a deal? I don't get it."

She shrugs, falling into step with me. "Wolf Ridge takes state in almost every sport. We're renowned. But Cole is special—he's entertainment on the field. Kinda toys with the other team. Like a cat with a mouse. It's legendary. So if he got benched for bad grades this week, everyone would've mourned. I know you had no choice, but you just became an unsung hero."

"I just became the laughing stock of the school and a target for every bully."

"Nah, just Cole."

"So do you have to be good at sports to be popular?"

"Yep." She sweeps her hands down her body with a giant rueful smile. "Guess you know why I won't get crowned homecoming queen."

I have the insane urge to steal the homecoming crown before it's given out this weekend just to give it to Rayne. And that thought makes me smile.

She elbows me. "It's not that funny."

My smile grows bigger. "I'm not laughing at you, I

swear. Just thinking how fun it would be to throw the contest."

She grins back. She leads me to the far side of the school, where there's a little patch of trees I hadn't seen before. "This is where I like to hide during lunch." She sinks down with her back against one of the trees.

I drop to join her. "This is way better than the places I've tried." It's true. She found the one tiny patch of real nature on campus where the air is somehow easier to breathe.

"So Cole thinks my mom stole his dad's job," I blurt, unable to keep my mind off it.

Rayne raises her brows. "You didn't know that?"

I sigh. Okay, Wolf Ridge *is* that small and interconnected. "I thought everyone hated me because I'm Hispanic."

She spits out her juice laughing. "That's hilarious."

"Well, it *is* pretty homogenous here. And I don't fit the bill. You should see the way Cole's dad stares out the window at us. I swear to God, I thought he or one of the other neighbors were going to call ICE on us, hoping we'd get picked up in the night just because our last name is Sanchez."

Rayne laughs so hard tears leak from the corners of her eyes. "No." She wipes at the moisture. "It's not racism you're combating here."

The way she draws out *racism* makes me think there's something else. Something besides my mom taking Cole's dad's job, but I can't for the life of me figure out what that would be.

She tucks a wild tuft of white-blonde hair behind her

ear, and I see the flash of a blue tattoo on the inside of her wrist. "What is that?" I ask, pointing to it.

She holds it out to show me a tiny paw print.

"Very sweet. Is it to remember a dog?"

"It's a wolf print, actually."

"Are wolves special to you?"

She quickly tucks it away and ducks her head. "No. Just for Wolf Ridge. It's stupid." She blushes furiously. "I wish I'd never gotten it, but it's too late now."

"I like it." An idea takes hold, one that gets me excited for the first time in months. A way to memorialize Catrina. "I want to get one. Did you get it here in town?"

"Yep. At Wolf's Paw Tattoo."

"Oh my God. Is that why you got a wolf's paw? Is it free if you become a walking advertisement for them?"

Rayne laughs. "No, but I guess that's where I got the idea, yeah. But you have to be eighteen or have parental consent."

"Well, it just so happens that my birthday is tomorrow." I grin. "Want to come with me?"

She lights up. "Definitely. What are you going to get inked?"

I swallow back the sudden lump in my throat. I guess I'm still not okay talking about it. Instead I shrug and go for mystery. "You'll see."

∾

COLE

. . .

"SERIOUSLY, I can't believe you made the human take your quiz for you." Wilde, our team captain, punches my shoulder in the locker room after showers. "That was so Gucci."

"Shut up with the Gucci thing, dude," Bo says. "You wouldn't know Gucci from Fruit of the Loom, asshole."

There's a chorus of snorts from the underclassmen, evidence of their continuous suck-up.

"Yeah, I figure Bailey Sanchez owes me a lot more than a passing grade on a pop quiz," I say.

Austin makes a dissenting sound beside me.

"What?" I demand.

He shrugs but looks away, acknowledging I'm alpha of this team and our group of friends, even if I'm not captain. Even if I'm not the biggest.

I'm definitely the meanest, and everyone knows it.

"Why is she even here?" Bo asks. "Brewery HR should've encouraged her mom to send her to Cave Hills with the rest of the humans."

I shake my head, the misery of the past few months washing over me. My dad's increased drinking. The way he picks fights with me and Casey. The progressive spiral of shit-tasticness. Things were bad before Bailey Sanchez arrived, but her moving in next door made them infinitely worse.

"I don't know, but I'm going to make her sorry for it."

"I don't know, I think she's kind of hot," Slade leers.

"Shut up, Slade," Austin warns. Slade's the oblivious one in our group. He's somehow missed that despite my intense dislike for Bailey, I also have a thing for her.

He goes on, though, oblivious to the warning, too.

18

"Nice tits and those little dresses. And those big eyes make her look just like a little Mexican doll—"

"Don't talk about her tits." I whirl and headbutt his face. There's a loud crunch of cartilage and bone.

He covers his nose. "Aw, fuck!"

Wilde and Bo jump between us in case there's more. Coach Jamison has a strict no fighting rule—one I've had a hard time with this year.

Like father, like son, I guess.

I lean to the left to look around Wilde's bulky frame and point a finger at Slade. "Don't mention her again. She's mine."

"What?" Slade still doesn't follow. "I thought you hated her."

"She's mine," I repeat firmly. "Mine to torment, and I'm going to enjoy the fuck out of it."

All four of my friends shake their heads like they're sorry for me.

"That's fucked up, dude," Austin says.

Slade finally realized he needs to keep his mouth shut. He shrugs and clicks the bones of his nose back in place. It will be healed by tomorrow; that's the glory of being a shifter.

"Speaking of HILFs"—humans I'd like to fuck—"you should see this chick from Cave Hills who showed up at the body shop yesterday." Bo whistles low, clearly trying to diffuse the tension. "Bangin' body with the attitude to match. She's trouble, though. I think the car she brought in to get painted was hot."

"Wait…" Slade says, finally coming up to speed and

ignoring Bo's far more interesting opener. "So you *do* want to fuck Bailey?"

It's a simple question. I'm not sure why the answer seems so complicated.

When I don't answer, Bo pipes in, "Why don't you just bone her if she's under your skin so bad? Get it out of your system."

Is that what I need? To hate-fuck the girl next door until she's out of my system?

Truth is, I never jacked off thinking about a human female. That is, until Bailey and her nerdy-hot body showed up.

She's got curves in all the right places, and that wide pink streak of hair she has does something to me. She acts like the straight A's goodie goodie, but that streak tells me she's a rebel at heart.

And Slade is right. The big dark eyes against smooth pale skin does make her look like a doll. A doll I want to do bad things to.

Maybe getting my hands on that juicy body of hers would be the cure for this shit. I can put her in her place while we both enjoy it.

I don't need her to move away; I need to get her beneath me. Need to hear her beg. Need her on her knees, mouth stuffed with my cock. Or tied up, face-down on my bed. Maybe on her back, my hand around her throat as I bang into that tight little cunt.

I guarantee she's a virgin.

She's way too perfect good-girl not to be.

Hmm. Ruining the daughter might be the perfect punishment for the human who took my dad's self-respect.

It's not a bad plan. I adjust my cock as the thought takes root and starts to spin.

"Hello? Cole?" Wilde waves a hand in front of my eyes. I guess I've been staring off.

"He's already boning her in his mind," Bo snorts.

"Yeah." I push my shoulder off the lockers. "I'm definitely planning on it."

"Just make it legal, dude, or Alpha Green will have your nuts. You know the rules," Austin warns.

Bile hits my throat. "Are you suggesting I'd *rape* her?" Anger makes my vision dome, my wolf showing his colors. I may be a dick, but do my own friends think I'd actually stoop that low?

There's no fucking way I stand for rape. Not ever. I have a little sister. I'd kill any fucker who forced himself on her. On any girl in this school. I may hate the girl, but shit. Wolves are protective by nature and there's a code of honor even I wouldn't ever stray from.

Austin takes a step back. So does Wilde. Bo jumps up off the bench and gives me wide berth, too.

"Whoa, sorry. Good. I just wanted to be sure." Austin has his hands up.

I turn away and yank my clothes on, still pissed.

"I'm sorry, dude. I definitely didn't mean—" Austin tries.

"Go fuck yourself."

"Yeah, okay. Fucking off. I'm still your best friend."

I flip him the bird over my shoulder. I know, very mature.

But calling BFF when we're seniors in high school is pretty juvenile, too. It's true. Austin's been my partner in

21

crime since we were pups and our moms taught at the elementary school together. And really, what he's saying is that he still has my back. No matter how dickish I get.

They all do. Because they know what's going down at my house.

And that's the only redeeming thing about pack living.

I grab my bag and head outside.

Casey's waiting for me, even though her practice is over an hour before mine. As a sophomore, my little sister is already star of the volleyball team, leading the school to what will be another state championship.

No cheerleader whores in this family, my dad likes to say. Which is a dig at our mom, who was cheer captain back when he was Wolf Ridge's defense star.

Casey climbs into the cab of the truck and slumps back, staring out the window. I start the truck and drive. We don't speak. We hardly acknowledge each other. This is our routine.

Casey could have caught a ride with any one of her friends. She doesn't have to wait for me to drive her home. But she does. And it's not because she wants to spend extra time with her big bro. Or because she just really likes to hang out after practice.

It's because she doesn't want to go home without me there to protect her.

ailey

GETTING a tattoo on the inside of my wrist hurts more than I expected. The artwork is exquisite: the iconic "Catrina" Day of the Dead skull is coming out exactly how I drew it, only better, because now it's forever inked on my body. Catrina's name is on a little banner below it.

But the pain. Holy crap. It's all I can do not to tear up while the guy works over my wrist, and my whole body's trembly and weak.

But it will be worth it. I needed to do something to memorialize her, and I hadn't figured out what until I saw Rayne's little paw print.

I sit in a chair in the front window of the little tattoo parlor. I guess they like to show their clients off to the world. Like I don't already feel like I'm living in a fishbowl in Wolf Ridge. Rayne lounges in another chair beside me, looking up funny YouTube videos to show me.

"Check this one out, it's the Google translated version of Billie Eilish's *Bad Guy*." She shoves her phone under my nose and I watch the parody, snorting at the badly interpreted lyrics like "*I'm a baaaaad cat*."

I smile through a wince. "I think I need something funnier."

"It really hurts you, huh?" Rayne eyes me with more curiosity than sympathy, which annoys me since I'm sweating from the pain.

"He's puncturing my skin over and over again with an ink-filled needle. Yeah it hurts. Did it not hurt when you got yours?"

She shrugs. "I don't remember."

The tattoo artist, Eric, a lanky, pierced guy with close-cropped hair and full sleeves of tats on both arms, exchanges a glance with Rayne like they're sharing some secret. Or agreeing I'm being a big wimp.

Maybe I am. I blow out my breath. I deserve this pain.

For Catrina.

"Uh oh." Rayne spins her chair around so the back faces the window. "Don't look now."

"What? Oh."

Fuck.

The WRH football team is jogging around the town square today. Lucky me.

"Excuse me?" I say to the tattoo artist. "Could we, um, face the other way?"

But it's too late. They are running past, and I see the

teammates' heads swiveling from me to Cole, who is in the middle of the pack. He catches sight of me and does a quick reverse step, nearly pulling the handle off the door with his momentum. Two of his buddies stop with him.

As he opens the door, one of them says, "Dude, no. Coach Jamison will kill us all if you disappear."

"I'll be right behind you." Cole's grin is wicked.

Butterflies flap panicked wings in my belly, smacking into my ribs and sending my pulse skyrocketing.

Cole saunters over. His muscles stretch his white t-shirt. He's hardly sweating, even though he was running in the afternoon sun. In Colorado it would be crispy fall by October, but apparently Arizona didn't get the autumn memo.

"It smells like pain in here." He saunters in my direction, gloating and glee radiating from every line of his athletic body. His brown eyes glitter. "Pain and"—he sniffs the air, then whirls suddenly to face Rayne—"fear." He lunges at her, gripping the two arm rests of the captain's chair and trapping her in it.

She squeaks.

He's right. She looks absolutely terrified.

"What are you doing here, Rayne-bow?"

She shrinks in her chair, eyes wide.

Anger flares and I get over my own sense of intimidation. "Get the fuck away from her," I snap.

He keeps her caged in, but slowly turns his face toward me. "Rayne-bow and Pink. I guess you two go together." He frowns though, and to my relief, pulls away from Rayne.

RENEE ROSE

I don't even care when he comes in my direction. I can handle him.

"What's up, Muchmore?" Eric mumbles, darting a sideways glance in Cole's direction. Great. Even the local business owners are intimidated by this high school punk.

Figures.

Cole crowds beside him, studying me. "You're in pain, Pink. Delicate little flower, aren't you?"

I roll my eyes. "It probably turns you on to see a person suffer, doesn't it?"

"Only you, Pink." He grins and squeezes his junk through his gym shorts.

I follow the motion with my gaze before I can stop myself. Oh lordy. He's got a big package, and yes... it is bulging.

And just like that, my body decides now is the time to bloom into womanhood. Again. I need to have a serious talk with my body and what it considers healthy sexual interactions. Teen hormones are the worst.

I mean, seriously, up to this point, I considered myself sort of asexual. I've kissed a few boys. Made out with a couple girls. Neither did much for me.

Right now, though, it's like a match just burst into flame in my core. Heat prickles across my skin. My nipples bead to painful little points.

And unfortunately, Cole doesn't miss it. His nostrils flare right before his gaze lands on my nips which are pointy even under my daisy trimmed lace bralette. "Who's turned on by suffering?" he mocks.

My face heats, comebacks eluding me as I become

26

even more acutely aware of the tightness of my breasts. The pulsing heat between my legs.

"Go to hell, Muchmore."

Yep, super mature.

Eric stops needling my skin and clears his throat, like he wants to say something to Cole, but doesn't quite have the nerve.

"Take a break," Cole orders and the spineless twit immediately backs away, leaving me totally exposed and alone for Cole's attack.

And attack he does, only it's not in the direction I expect.

He leans in, gripping the arms of my chair like he did with Rayne. "It's good you like pain, little flower. Because I plan to make you suffer."

It's a threat, but his eyes are heavy-lidded. Like he's in sexual ecstasy at the thought.

And for some reason, my body keeps responding to his nearness. The thrum between my legs matches my heartbeat.

He leans in even closer, so close I think he's going to bite me or something, but all he does is inhale deeply, his nose at the side of my neck.

When he pulls back, his eyes look weird. Like more gold than brown. He gives a sharp shake of his head and exhales. Snatches my hand up and examines the ink, like he's using it as a distraction.

"Little Miss Perfect is getting a tattoo? I can't believe it."

I'm too flustered to answer. Too off-center. Too vulnerable.

"I wouldn't think your straight-laced mom would sign the permission form to let her perfect little girl get marked up."

"She's eighteen today," Rayne offers.

I would glare at her, but I'm too busy studying Cole's eyes, which now appear to be back to brown. Had I just imagined them turning gold? I must have.

Cole's brows shoot up. "This is your birthday deed, huh? You were chomping at the bit to get inked?"

I don't know why his interest causes such a sideways shifting in my chest. I try to pull my wrist back, but he doesn't release it.

"What is this? A skull?" He cocks his head at me, examining my face, then returning to study the artwork. "Some kind of Mexican heritage thing?" Again, he looks at my face. "Or did someone die?"

I swear I didn't show anything, but he goes still. "Who died, Pink?"

This time I do manage to yank my hand back. "Get out of here, Cole." I choke. Unwelcome grief bubbles up to the surface, and I sure as hell don't want to break down in front of my worst enemy.

I'm saved by his two football buddies pushing the door open.

"Cole, move it. Coach hasn't noticed yet, but he's going to," Wilde, the biggest one says. I think he's captain of the football team. Definitely another superstar alpha-hole at WRH.

Cole slowly backs up, still raking me over with his gaze. Then he turns and walks out with his friends, taking all the oxygen from the room with him.

I can't manage to suck in a breath until they're out of sight, around the corner.

"Huh," Rayne says.

"What?"

Eric shuffles back toward me and resumes his work as if nothing happened. This time, I hardly notice the pain.

"I think you have more power with Cole Muchmore than you think."

My gut clenches, nerves still raw. "What do you mean, *more power*?"

She looks thoughtfully out the window in the direction the boys disappeared. "It's true he can't stand you. But that doesn't mean he doesn't want to get you horizontal."

I wish my reaction to that news was revulsion, but instead, lightning zings through my core and a shiver runs through me. Eric tightens his grip on my hand to keep me from screwing up the tattoo, then shoots a look at Rayne that for some reason reads as a warning.

He's warning her not to distract me? Or not to encourage me to tangle with Cole?

It's not like I plan to.

But if Rayne's right? If Cole Muchmore wants me? That changes everything. If it's true, I do hold a shred of power. And I can use it as a weapon…

COLE

BAILEY and the defective little runt Rayne.

29

That's a combination I wouldn't have ever put together. I nearly made Rayne pee herself over breaking my school-wide edict of not befriending the human, but the truth is, I don't give a shit. If Pink wants to be friends with the lowest kid in the pack, that's fine. She probably needs someone to talk to.

Something about it irritates me, though. Rayne's not good enough for Pink. She's like two or three years younger and a friendless nobody. Pack dynamic demands it be that way. If Pink were at a human school, she'd be in a strata close to the top, considering she's librarian-hot. She wouldn't be hanging out with a kid like Rayne.

I kind of loved the way Pink protected the runt, though. It's funny to see humans display the same alpha protection of friends that packs rely on. They probably don't even understand the biology beneath it. But Pink has backbone, I'll give her that.

I run back to the field, mulling over Pink's new ink. Turns out there's more depth to the hot nerd than I noticed. She lost someone, too. She has a wound.

Some might think it would make me want to pour salt and lemon juice all over it, but it doesn't.

She's already broken.

She already knows pain.

Somehow that satisfies the angriest part of me. Like it levels the field between us.

Doesn't mean I don't still want to take her down a few notches. Get her under me. Begging me. Calling my name. Eager to give me anything, everything, I want.

I give my head a shake. Just the thought makes my step lighter.

I think that may be all I need. To fuck the human.

Once I've conquered Bailey—once I've broken her myself—then I can let this go.

BAILEY

I WASN'T PLANNING on going to the homecoming game. I don't even know why I'm here.

Because Rayne talked me into it, I guess.

We sit way in the back, where we still have to squeeze to get seats.

I swear, the entire town showed up for this game. People are all dressed in blue and white, waving signs and pom-pons.

"Welcome Wolf Ridge!" Austin, student council president and one of the football alpha-holes, stands in the middle of the field with a microphone. "Before the game, we'll be announcing the homecoming royalty."

"Dammit, I wanted to steal you that crown," I mutter to Rayne, who laughs. She's been giving me the inside scoop on everyone around us—the who's who of Wolf Ridge.

"From the junior class, the prince is Alex Shank." The crowd cheers as one of the football players jogs up to get his crown. "And junior class princess... Chiara Deane!" More whoops and cheers. "And our senior class king is..." His dramatic pause goes on too long and the crowd starts stomping and cheering. "Cole Muchmore!"

"Ugh," I groan. "Like he needs the boost to his ego."

"Actually, he might," Rayne says, reminding me of his dad's unemployment which sends a stab of guilt through me.

"And the queen is… Adriana Drake!"

I have no opinion about Adriana Drake, the blonde cheerleader who dashes out to the field to get her crown. That is until she throws her arms around Cole's neck like they're announcing their engagement. Then I decide she's a conceited bitch without brains who probably doesn't even know how to tie her own shoes.

"Oh that's cute," Rayne says dryly. "They dated last year. Looks like the student body wants to see them together again."

My stomach cramps, a hot ball of something that's not jealousy lodging in my chest.

I'm not jealous.

Definitely not jealous.

Why would I be jealous of someone dating Cole? I should welcome his distraction from making my life a living hell.

Reasoning with myself doesn't help, though. I can't stand the cheerleader I already decided is a bitch. She gets her crown but stays glued to Cole, one arm wrapped around his waist.

It's hard to tell from where we're sitting, but his posture looks bored and impatient, though maybe that's what I want to see.

Dammit.

I seem to be getting as obsessed about my tormentor as he is with me.

The royalty leaves the field and the band plays a couple numbers.

The cheerleaders and pom-pon girls make two lines outside the stadium doors where the team comes out and lift their shivering pom-pons overhead to make a tunnel.

The crowd gets on their feet cheering for the grand entrance.

"Woo hoo, you ran out on a field," I mock in a voice only Rayne can hear.

She elbows me in the ribs. "Get in the spirit. Games are fun."

Games are fun.

Okay. I'll have to take her word for it.

I scan the players. They all look the same in their big shoulder pads and helmets.

"Number twenty-six," Rayne says.

"What?"

"That's Cole's number. You were looking for him, right?"

My face grows hot. "Nope."

She grins. "Liar."

I find twenty-six and instantly wonder how I didn't recognize him. Cole struts out on the field with that predatory grace, making the rest of the team look like lumbering idiots.

The coin is tossed. The teams line up. The other team gets the ball.

I watch the game with less interest in the actual sport, although I am fairly fascinated by the prowess of one quarterback in particular, but more as an anthropological study.

Sports have replaced battle in our culture. They're a

proving ground for young warriors—part of young people's rite of passage into adulthood. What else can we do with these amazing physical abilities we no longer need in today's society? Use it or lose it in evolution, right?

I have to admit I'm impressed by the beauty of the dance out on the field. And truly, Wolf Ridge High's players are ten times better than the other team's. More coordinated, stronger, bigger.

Just better.

I can see why sports are big here.

At halftime, I brave the crowds to buy some nachos. Rayne sticks by my side, although she darts nervous glances at the people around us.

"Do you hate big crowds?" I ask to ease her tension. "I do."

"Um, yeah. Totally." She gnaws on her lip, and I get the feeling there's more to it.

While I'm waiting for the nachos, the homecoming queen cuts into the line. What's her name? Oh yeah... *Adriana.*

She catches sight of me and gives me the once-over, then does the same to Rayne. Her lip curls. "What are you doing with the new girl, Rayne?" There's venom and accusation in her voice, and it sends chills up and down my spine.

I remember what Cole said to her in the tattoo shop: *What are you doing here?*

Was there some rule about no one befriending me?

No, that's nuts. I'm being way too paranoid.

But Adriana advances on Rayne, crowding into her with a level of physical intimidation I'm not used to seeing in girls. "I'm serious. What. Do you think. You're doing?"

I grab Rayne and pull her behind me. She may be small, but that doesn't mean people can push her around.

"Back off, princess." I eye her crown, fantasizing about ripping it off her head and breaking it. Or better yet, putting it on Rayne's head. I'm not the type to get into altercations—ever—but I swear the culture at this school is all about aggression and intimidation, and I'm not going to tuck my tail and run this time. I'm done staying quiet while everyone acts like asswipes.

Adriana lets out a sound that resembles a growling dog.

It's not attractive.

"Don't." Rayne pulls my arm with urgency. "Seriously, walk away. Come on."

It's only because Rayne's alarm seems so genuine that I let her tug me away. It seems like it goes beyond social discomfort and into real fear, and that disturbs me.

We get some distance between us before I remember my nachos.

"Leave them," Rayne says. Her eyes are still wide and frightened. "Seriously. Don't start trouble with those girls. You could get hurt."

"Like... physically hurt?"

She nods rapidly. "Yeah."

My stomach turns over. Jesus. This town just gets weirder and weirder. Its vibe is somewhere between *Deadly Class* and the 1990s horror movie *Disturbing Behavior*.

There may have been a few mean girls at my old high

school, but I don't think kids were quaking in fear over getting beat up. That's a problem that needs to be rectified. Like the culture here needs to change.

"I was hungry," I complain.

"Come on," Rayne says. "There's a Dairy Queen on the corner. We can walk over."

I'd just as soon head home, but since I don't drive anymore and I told my mom to pick me up at ten, it's not an option. Besides, I don't want to leave Rayne in the lurch. Seems like she needs my friendship as much as I need hers.

Also, Oreo Blizzards go a long way toward fixing most problems.

We stay for the entire second half of the game, not walking back until we hear the victory cheers echo from the stadium.

By the time we get to the parking lot, it's empty of over half the cars carrying parents and families, and teeming with kids from school getting into every kind of trouble you can imagine. There's a full-on bare knuckle brawl going on in one corner, the scent of pot wafting through the air. One group openly passes a huge bottle of vodka around their semicircle, taking pulls of it and handing it over to the next person like it's a joint.

Cole Muchmore leans against his antique Ford, wearing a ripped t-shirt and jeans. His hair looks wet, like he's fresh out of the shower. His main accessory is the cheerleader trying to climb him.

Adriana, the homecoming queen.

I don't want to look—I swear I don't—but I find myself staring as we go by.

I'm probably reading more into it than I should, but it looks like he's trying to push her away—is annoyed by her attempts to consummate their royal marriage.

And then he sees me. The moment he does, I know I'm fucked. There's so much glee. The promise of punishment. My steps falter. Our gazes lock.

He wraps his fist in the back of Adriana's hair and pushes her down, forcing her to her knees in front of his crotch. Apparently she's desperate enough to oblige his vulgar suggestion, because she mouths him through his jeans, biting at the bulge there.

Shock ripples through me.

Disgust.

Heat.

Crows of encouragement pepper the air from the other boys around, their jeers making Adriana bolder.

I don't want to watch—I don't. Rayne tugs at my arm, but I'm glued to the dirt, unable to look away.

My nipples pucker, pussy flutters.

I shouldn't find this debasement hot.

He's cruel with her, still holding her hair, a sneer curling his lips.

The crowd catches on that it's about me. That his gaze is on me.

Adriana's friends call to her. Cole's start muttering.

Adriana looks up at him, sees his focus and whips around to look at me. Outrage flames across her face.

Cole releases her hair and she falls to the dirt on her butt. He chuckles, still watching me, and grabs his junk.

I shake my head.

For some reason, my heart pounds in my chest like I just ran a lap around the football field.

"Bailey, *come on*," Rayne urges, pulling harder. "Don't let him screw with your head."

Adriana scrambles to her feet and shoves Cole, hard. He just smirks. When she whirls on me, I realize I should've taken off when I had the chance.

Especially considering the warning Rayne already gave me about her.

Cole catches her arm, though, causing her to rubber-band back at him. He says something to her that sounds a lot like, "Leave it. She's mine."

My feet come unglued.

Rayne and I take off running toward the street, away from all the party and mayhem.

Away from Cole Muchmore and the alpha-hole football heroes.

Away from his words.

Away from his claim on me.

She's mine.

He's wrong. All wrong.

But no matter how fast I run, no matter how far I go, his words still chase me. The image of his face still taunts me. And when I close my eyes to go to sleep tonight, I know it will be my hair he's tangling in his fist. Not Adriana's. It'll be me kneeling before him. Not her. Me.

Cole

. . .

"LEAVE IT. SHE'S MINE."

Adriana splutters in my face, fire sparking in her eyes. It occurs to me that Bailey could be in real danger, the kind a human wouldn't recover from quickly.

The kind that could leave permanent scars and necessitate a trip to the ER.

"You'll leave the human the fuck alone."

Adriana gapes in outrage when I infuse my words with alpha command.

"You're defending *it*, now?" She refers to Bailey as an *it*, like being a human is less than nothing. Everyone is fucking watching us. Listening. Waiting to hear my reply.

I want to tell them all Bailey is under my protection. I may be hellbent on getting under Bailey's skin, but I'm not going to set her up to get attacked. And that's the only reason I feel this fierce, almost violent urge to protect her right now. But if I admit she's under my protection, everyone will think I like her. It's bad enough my best friends and teammates know I want to bone down with the human. I don't need the whole school thinking I caught feeling.

"No, I just don't think she's worth getting called before Alpha Greene and the council for."

"And that's the only reason?"

"Of course, babe," I murmur in a conspiratorial tone. "You really think I want some bitch, when I can have you? The Queen of Wolf Ridge High."

That catches her attention.

I pull her face a little closer to mine. "Thanks for helping me fuck with the human. Did you see her expression?" I don't know why it sickens me slightly to share my genuine satisfaction with Adriana, but it does.

Whatever. It works. A slow smile splits Adriana's cheeks. "I did." She drags the last word out, trailing her fingertip over my collarbone.

I grit my teeth and reward her with a kiss, open-mouthed and sloppy for everyone to see.

I'm a cold bastard to use Adriana, but she's the one who was using me first. Just because we both got crowned royalty—*ridiculous*—doesn't mean we're going to rekindle the old flame.

And it's not like there was a real flame to begin with. I always consider her a dodged bullet. We hooked up once at a party up on the mesa. There was liquor involved which doesn't impair shifters as much as humans, except when the moon is full.

The moon was full.

Our hormones were raging.

Kids were shifting and running and getting naked all over the place. We went all the way.

Dangerous territory for shifter teens. There's a reason young males are subtly encouraged to sow their wild oats away from the pack, with humans.

For one thing, no kid is alpha enough to think he can face the angry daddy wolf and not suffer serious permanent consequences. Fathers are hella protective of their baby girls in this town. And fate forbid you get a girl pregnant. You can kiss any hope of finding your one true mate goodbye. You will be bound to that girl for the rest of your life, whether either of you want it or not.

That's what happened to my parents. At least the way my mom told it to me before she abandoned us.

So yeah. I didn't sleep for a month after it happened until Adriana told me we were in the clear.

And I've had nothing to do with her since.

I know she doesn't give a shit about me, either; she was just putting on a show to raise her status even more after the crowning.

Which is why I used her to get a rise out of Pink.

And pinken she did. A pretty rose color that lit up her pale cheeks and made those dark eyes brighter. I bet if I was close enough, I would've smelled that same sweet arousal she leaked when she was sitting in the chair at the tattoo parlor.

I want to get rough with her.

This isn't the cold dish of revenge some adversaries prefer.

No, there's a blazing hot undercurrent that runs through every interaction I have with that girl.

Seeing her blush—punishing her through humiliation and her own desire—gets me hard.

And I have no plans of backing off, because I haven't felt any kind of pleasure at all in a long time.

Since before my dad lost his job.

Before he started drinking.

After… After my mom left and my dad took consolation in a bottle. After my family slowly fell apart, the pain was like a sharp knife turning in my heart. Any way I moved, any action I took, thought I followed, I still felt it.

But this heat Pink produces in me? It flushes away some of the pain. Dulls it. No—transmutes it.

Rage and rebellion still simmer, but every time I get close to her, it's like the excitement of a full moon. The promise of something dark and satisfying if I follow my urge to punish her by claiming her fully.

Because she's human and there's a natural imbalance of power—even if she doesn't know it—I get wickedly high knowing how easy it will be to dominate her.

"Hey, kids," Bo's older brother Winslow strolls up with a couple of his buddies. He's an alum of Wolf Ridge, graduated a couple years ago and works at his uncle's body shop, where Bo and I work on weekends.

He's a dick.

Still wishes he was in high school. He's in full swagger mode, carrying a six-pack of beer in each hand. "Not a bad game, but you could've played down the first half a little more." He tucks one six-pack under his arm and starts breaking the cans off the rings and tossing them to the football players.

Because we play against humans, half the art for us is making our wins look natural. Losing a little so when we show off, it looks like some spectacular come back. Or freak luck.

It's stupid, but it entertains the whole town. Shifters are physical creatures. Physical prowess is glorified here. Physical aggression respected. Physical punishment is the norm. You offend someone, you'll probably get hurt. Which is no big deal, because we heal overnight.

Still, Winslow and his buddies are dangerous, especially when they've been drinking, and we all shift around, keeping gazes lowered and murmuring our agreement in case they came here spoiling for a fight.

"Now where are those cheerleaders?" Winslow's buddy Ben asks. He's definitely drunk. He tosses Adriana over his shoulder.

Fuck.

"Oh yeah, I'll take two," Winslow chortles and grabs the two girls nearest him and throws one over each shoulder.

The girls scream and kick. I hear some giggling. But Adriana looks like she's really fighting. Maybe Marcy is, too, I can't be sure.

Bo and I exchange an uneasy glance.

We can't directly challenge these assholes. They are bigger and stronger than we are. Plus, they think they're hot shit because they're older, so any confrontation will be taken as a vie for a change in pack order, which will bring out violent instincts. Not a good mix when drinking's involved.

"Hey, Ben, did you catch that Sun Devil game last week?"

He whirls to face me, making Adriana scream. She's kicking hard and punching at his kidneys, but he doesn't seem to notice. "Yeah, what about it?"

I'm thinking fast, trying to remember anything at all interesting about the ASU game. "That Gary Jones shows promise, don't you think?"

It works.

Ben drops Adriana on her feet to face me. "Gary Jones? Are you kidding? The asshole doesn't have a scrap of talent."

Adriana glares furiously at his back as he launches into his explanation of who on the team is worth watching.

After a few seconds Winslow loses interest in the girls he picked up, too, and unceremoniously dumps them to join in the conversation.

Bo steps in to close the ranks and solidify the sports talk.

The rest of the group disperses, trying not to make it too obvious they're getting away to find a better—and more private—place to party.

Bo and I stay and keep the conversation going, taking one for the team.

I shake my head. Same story different night.

Fucking pack living.

CHAPTER 4

 *ailey*

JOURNALISM CLASS—THE one where I sit beside Cole—becomes the source of all kinds of anxiety and anticipation over the next week. It used to be my favorite. I don't know, maybe it still is. Mr. Brumgard likes me. He makes a special effort to engage with me. I'd like to think it's because of my interest in the subject and because I'm a great student, not because he pities me. Not because he sees how left out I am at this school, how ostracized.

Now, though, I think about the class all day, get cold sweats before I go in, and flutters every time I see Cole out of the corner of my eye.

I never look at him directly.

I don't want to invite more attention.

Except, that's not true, because I have all kinds of

fantasies of having a normal conversation with him. Or of him showing interest.

And he does.

Show interest.

I feel his searing stares all period long, but he has yet to say anything or initiate any conversation.

Today is no different. His long legs fill the aisle between us, jutting toward me and my desk, crossed casually at the ankles. I have no doubt the infringement on my space is deliberate. I try not to stare at the size of his shoes, but damn. They're huge. He's already six feet tall and I'll bet he's not done growing.

He rocks his foot back and forth like he knows I'm looking at it.

"I hope you all took a look at the assigned reading." Brumgard passes papers out, face down.

The class groans, recognizing the cues for another pop quiz.

I did the reading, so I'm not worried, but I can't help but dart a glance at Cole.

Big mistake. He's staring at me with those fathomless dark eyes.

Just staring. I can't read anything in his expression.

Then he lifts his chin just slightly.

A question.

I shake my head.

The corner of one lip curls up, like he's amused by my defiance. Like he knows I'm going to cave and help him anyway.

I look back to the front of the room, still shaking my head.

"You may begin," Brumgard says.

I flip my test over, this time writing my name in the blank line on the top first. Can't fool me twice.

The answers are easy if you read the material, and I finish in less than a minute.

And then I doodle on my page.

Stare at the blemishes on my desk. The ink stains, the carved letters, the scratches.

I look up at Brumgard, who is pacing around the room. I don't know why he doesn't just sit at his desk where he can see the whole class at the same time. It's like he's inviting people to cheat.

Dammit, I give in and glance at Cole.

He flicks his brows.

My heart beats faster. But then my pulse has been elevated from the moment I tangled in his gaze.

Don't do it.

Do *not* do it.

Keeping my eyes on Brumgard's back, I tip my exam up and angle it so Cole can see the answers.

Seriously, I must've taken stupid pills this morning. What am I doing? Am I so desperate for Cole to not hate me that I'm willing to screw up my future? Screw up with the teacher who likes me best at this school?

Nausea rolls through me and the paper trembles. Which means Cole can see how badly my hand's shaking.

Damn him.

No, damn *me*. I'm choosing to risk my grade, my reputation, the recommendations I plan to ask for. All for a chance to get sneered at again by the alpha-hole next door.

Ridiculous.

Brumgard calls time and collects the tests. I manage not to look over at Cole. It's a minute-by-minute test, but I make the entire rest of the class without giving in to the urge.

After class, I wait by Mr. Brumgard's desk with the folder of recommendation forms. "Mr. Brumgard?"

He glances at the folder in my hand and reaches for it with a smile.

"Hi. These are recommendation forms. For college?"

He nods, his eyes crinkling with warmth. "I'd be happy to write a recommendation for you, Bailey. And listen, I've been thinking—about the student newspaper."

There's no school newspaper at Wolf Ridge High. I approached Mr. Brumgard at the beginning of the year to ask if he'd be willing to lead one as a club but he said no one would join—the only after-school thing kids at WRH cared about was sports.

I'm distinctly aware of the fact that Cole is also still in the classroom, ostensibly tying his shoe. I have a feeling he's actually making sure I'm not telling on him about the quiz.

"Yes?"

"Are you still interested?"

I perk up. This is the first bone anyone at WRH has thrown me. "Totally."

"I can assign stories in class as part of the coursework. And you could work with me after school putting it together. How does that sound?"

"I'd love to," I breathe, excited about schoolwork for the first time since I came to Wolf Ridge. Finally a challenge. Something to work for.

"Great. Come by after school today and we can start planning it."

"Today? Oh, yeah. Okay, that works."

I have no idea how I will get home after the bus leaves, but I'm sure I can figure it out. This is important.

I turn around, only to bump straight into Cole loitering behind me.

"Do you need something, Cole?" Brumgard asks.

"Yeah, I need to talk to you about extra credit. You know, to bring my grade up for—"

"For the game Saturday?" Brumgard gives a long-suffering sigh.

I leave before I hear the rest of the conversation, but I can guarantee Cole wasn't worried about his grade; he was making sure I didn't rat on him.

And I probably should have.

I don't know why I want to be on Team Cole when he is so set on being against Team Bailey.

I rub the tattoo on the inside of my wrist. Somehow, this is all tied into tragedy. My guilt for Catrina warped into a need to atone with Cole. It's illogical, but I've yet to have a logical, coinciding thought and feeling when it comes to Cole Muchmore.

~

BAILEY

. . .

49

MR. BRUMGARD IS in his classroom after school. He greets me with a smile. "Hi, Bailey, come on in." He pulls out a chair beside him, behind the desk. "Have a seat."

I sit down, fighting the awkwardness of working directly with an adult. I'm excited about this project, but nervous, too.

Mr. Brumgard smiles at me. "I'm glad you're interested in a student newspaper, Bailey. I think it's a great idea."

I suck my lower lip between my teeth and nod.

"The culture at Wolf Ridge is strange, as you've probably noticed. A lot of emphasis is on sports, and not much on anything academic. You're one of the very few students interested in even applying for college. While the graduation rate is decent here, the number of students who continue their studies is less than ten percent. No one leaves Wolf Ridge."

"Yeah, I've definitely noticed. My mom's friends at work all told her I should go to Cave Hills instead, but I don't drive, so it's too far."

Brumgard studies me. "Yes, Cave Hills would've been a much better choice for you. Although on the upside, you're probably a shoo-in for valedictorian here. First quarter grades have you at the very top of the senior class."

Pleasure floods my chest. I know it's geeky, but achievement has always been my thing. My mom says I get it from my dad, who died in Afghanistan when I was a baby, but I think it's just as much from her. I was raised to work hard and earn the accolades. I know for most kids that sounds like the opposite of fun, but for me, it's everything.

Brumgard touches my shoulder. I ignore the creeping tingles it gives me. "I can see you're having a hard time fitting in, Bailey. I want you to know that my door is always open if you need a friend."

The words are kind. Probably what I've been wanting to hear, but somehow they don't strike me as sincere. There's something off, but I'm not sure what. Like he's trying to manipulate me for something.

But that doesn't make sense.

"Honestly, sometimes I wonder if the families in Wolf Ridge are in some kind of closed religious community. Mormons, maybe," Brumgard says.

I shoot him a dubious look, thinking of Cole's dad with a beer bottle in his hand every time I see him. "With most of the population employed by a brewery? Definitely not." Mormons don't drink.

"Well, some kind of cult, then."

Huh. A cult.

The town doesn't strike me as particularly religious, but there *is* something cultish about it. Goosebumps race up my arms.

Could that be why I'm such an outsider here? I'm not part of their cult?

But what kind of cult could it be? Sports-worship?

I make a non-committal sound.

"Anyway, I'd like you to brainstorm a list of articles you want to run in the first edition of the paper, and write them on the board. We can go over them together and then I'll assign them to the class tomorrow."

I get up from my seat, happy to no longer be so close to Brumgard. I already had ideas for articles, although I don't know if I can come up with thirty-some different ideas for each kid in class.

I pick up a dry-erase marker and start putting my ideas up. I brainstorm a "teacher of the week" quiz featuring a different teacher without revealing his or her identity. Students can turn in their answers for a chance to win a prize. Coverage of all the sports. Those should be easy, and in fact, could take up most of the newspaper if I can't come up with other ideas. Features on clubs. News reporting on upcoming or past events like the homecoming royalty, the dance this weekend, all that.

I keep at it for forty-five minutes, filling the board with my ideas. When I run out of steam, Brumgard swivels in his chair and looks it over. "Come on over here and tell me about each of those," he says, beckoning me toward him.

Later I would wonder why I was so stupid. I registered the warning signs on some level, but didn't bring them into my consciousness.

I trot obediently over to him and stand beside his chair as I verbally walk him through my thought process on each article.

And that's when it happens.

It's so unexpected, I almost can't assimilate it at first.

Mr. Brumgard's hand slides up my inner thigh.

I freeze. Ice and fire rush through me at once. My stomach hurls into my ribs, trapping my breath.

Later I would wish I'd done a million things.

Gone kung fu on his ass. Stepped quickly back. Throat-punched him. Yelled, *get your fucking hands off me!*

But I don't do any of them.

I just stay frozen as his sweaty palm moves higher until it meets my crotch and he rubs his fingers over my panties.

And then my brain completely disconnects. I'm at total odds with what *should be* happening and what is *actually* happening. The room spins.

I'm going to puke.

When his fingers prod under my panties, I stiffen up like a board.

Blackness creeps in around my vision as it narrows to a single spot on the desk.

COLE

AFTER PRACTICE, I throw my gym bag and backpack in the truck. Casey isn't around, she texted me she has a group project she's working on with Stacy, but there's a prickle on the back of my neck like I need to be aware of something.

Wolf sense coming through.

I sniff the air.

Nothing.

I look back at the school. The light's still on in Brumgard's room.

Fucking Bailey. She's in there playing teacher's pet, working on her precious newspaper project. Am I getting prickly because she's turning me in for cheating?

Never one to miss an opportunity to throw her off balance, I slam the truck door and head back to the school.

Brumgard told me to stop by and pick up my graded papers to rewrite them, so I have a perfect excuse to show up, anyway.

Most of the outside doors are locked now, but I find an open one and jog through the halls, a sense of urgency pushing me forward.

When I open the door to the classroom, I'm totally unprepared for what I see.

Actually, scent comes first: The salty smell of tears and behind it—fear. Shame. Anger.

Next, sight. Brumgard has his hand up Bailey's skirt. Pink appears frozen in shock. She's white as a ghost and looks like she's about to vomit.

And that's when I lose my shit. I hurtle across the room, closing the distance between me and him.

One punch—shifter strength—and his head snaps back, blood spurts from his nose. The chair he sat on flies back and hits the wall with Brumgard still in it.

I go in for more. I'm ready to kill the fucker, but Bailey wakes up from her stupor, grabs her backpack and tears out of the room.

"Bailey!" I shout.

I'm torn between the need to punish this asshole adult who touched her—fucking *touched her* against her will— and wanting to follow Bailey and make sure she's okay.

I point a damning finger at Brumgard. "You ever fucking touch her or another student, and you're a dead man. Understand?"

Our teacher makes some kind of moaning sound from where he's crumpled on the floor, blood streaming from his face. I don't think his neck is broken, but I definitely hit him hard enough it could've happened. He's lucky he's alive. He's lucky I'm letting him live.

I back out of the room and run.

There's no sign of Bailey in either direction.

Fuck!

I take the first exit and scan the parking lot. I still don't see her. Jogging to the truck, I jump in and start it, then take off to loop around the school.

There I see her in the back, running.

I screech the tires pulling up next to her. "Bailey! Get in the truck."

She ignores me. She's sobbing so hard as she runs I'm surprised she can even see where she's going.

I reach across and throw the passenger door open as I step on the gas to keep pace with her. "Bailey, hold up! Get in the truck, I'll drive you home."

"Leave me alone!"

I throw the truck in neutral and pull on the parking brake, then jump out my side. I catch her from behind as she stumbles over a crack in the sidewalk and lift her feet off the ground. She goes wild in my arms, punching and kicking.

"Hey, it's okay. Bailey."

"Shut up, Cole."

"I'll shut up. You get in the fucking truck." I infuse my words with alpha command, even though she's not a shifter.

On some level, humans relate to it.

It works.

She stops struggling and dashes the back of her hand across her eyes. "Fine." If I were less disturbed about what just went down, I would celebrate that little victory. Same as I celebrated her showing me her quiz today.

She surrenders to me despite her better judgment.

I stay close behind her in case she decides to bolt again, but she climbs in and slams the door, then stares straight ahead.

I get back in and throw the truck in gear. Now what? I hadn't thought further than getting to Bailey.

The principal is gone for the day. We could go back and talk to him tomorrow. But this can't wait.

I ease my foot off the clutch and get on the road.

"You okay?" It's a dumb question. Of course she's not okay.

"Peachy," she snaps.

I rub the back of my neck. She's definitely not. I scent shame and fear on her.

"Don't feel ashamed." I say it like a command, not a suggestion. Make my voice firm. "You didn't do anything wrong. You know that, right?"

She's silent for a moment. "I feel so fucking dirty." Her voice is full of tears again.

"Yeah, well you're not. He is." I shut up after that, though. She doesn't need to talk to me. She needs a friend.

Still, I'm unwilling to let her out of my sight until we've had a conversation.

Plus, Brumgard needs to be thrown out of this town on his ass. I pull up in front of the sheriff's office and Pink stiffens.

"What are we doing here?"

"We're going to go in there and tell them what happened and you're going to press charges."

She shakes her head; tears start making silent trails down her cheeks again.

Fuck. I knew this wouldn't be easy.

"Why not?"

She strangles the strap of her backpack with her hand. "I'm not up for this. I just need to think. I want to go home."

Shit. This isn't right. Brumgard needs to be stopped. If he tried this with Pink, he's probably done it before and will do it again.

"You can't let him get away with this, Bailey. Taking him down is the right thing to do. And it will be so easy. You had a witness. How many girls can say that? It will be an easy conviction."

She doesn't say anything, but I scent her resistance and despair like burnt rubber. I don't like being the cause of that scent.

"You're not in this alone. I'd be a part of it the whole way through. I'll tell the story. All you have to do is press charges."

"I can't, Cole. I mean I'll think about it. I know you're right, but I just can't face this right now. I'm already the weird girl at school. I can't take any more negative attention."

Fuck. That part is my fault.

I curse and put the truck back in gear. Ultimately, it's her call.

I can't take her home, though. Instead, I drive around to the back side of the mesa, to a place I like to go when I need to get away. And I figure Pink needs to think right now.

I pull down the dirt road and park in a long-forgotten parking lot overgrown with creosote.

"Where are we?"

"Come on. I'll show you." For a moment, I wonder if I've made a mistake bringing her here. She just got blind-sided by a teacher's sexual advances, I don't want her to think I have something nefarious in mind, too. But I don't scent fear from her.

Still, I don't breathe until she swings the door open and hops out.

Her face softens as she looks around. "What is this place?"

We duck through a continuous archway formed by at least a dozen out-of-control palo verde trees and emerge in the clearing framed on one side by a fifty foot canyon wall.

"What is this place?" There's awe in her tone.

The bones of a stone building that once served as a picnic ramada stand off to one side, the roof long since caved in or removed. The giant picnic table is still inside, though, gouged by at least a hundred sets of initials carved in the thick, smooth wood.

I don't know what I love so much about this place. The archeology of a modern ruin, I guess. The way it's hidden back in here under the giant cottonwoods and overgrown mesquite and palo verde. The way it's protected by the secret canyon.

No humans come here anymore. It doesn't show up on any map. Alpha Green somehow arranged for the pack to buy this park from the city of Wolf Ridge years ago.

"Was it a playground?" She takes in the old rusty swing set, merry-go-round and teeter totter.

"Yep. An old one. Hasn't been used since the 70s. I don't know why they didn't remove the equipment. It's probably uber-dangerous." I plunk down on one of the swings to prove how much I love danger.

She sits on the one beside me and pushes with her feet to make it sway.

I climb off mine and grab her waist, pulling her back. "Maybe they didn't have these things in Colorado." I speak slowly, like I'm explaining something profound. "But you actually *swing* with them." I push her hips, sending her sailing high into the air.

She shrieks a little, but laughs. "Jesus, you're strong."

Oops. I make a note to dial back the shifter strength.

Nah, fuck it. Why not show off a little?

I push her again, sending the chains of the swing so high they're parallel to the ground.

She screams when she catches a little air before falling back into the seat.

I chuckle.

We stay like that for a while—me pushing, her soaring through the air, hanging on to the swing for dear life. I didn't think this through, but now that we're here, I'm glad. It feels right.

After a while, I stop pushing and let the momentum die.

I stroll over to the merry-go-round. "Ever been on one of these?"

She shakes her head.

"I'm not surprised. They outlawed them long before we were born. Way too dangerous. And all of this shit made out of metal? I bet a whole lot of kids in the 70s were covered in third degree burns in the summer."

"Oh my God, you're right. It's way too hot in Arizona for metal equipment." She hops off the swing and comes toward me.

I hold out my hand and help her onto the wobbly metal saucer. "Ready?"

"I doubt it," she says, but a smile plays around her lips. I'm so fucking relieved to see it there, I just smile back.

I've forgotten all the animosity between us. My need to punish her. It's not that I still don't want to master her —I do.

It's more that I want her whole when I succeed.

"Hang on," I warn before giving the handlebars a shove. The equipment is rusty, so it takes me a while to get it going, but once I do, I put a little shifter strength into it and the wheel flies around.

Bailey screams, her long dark hair flying around her face, her eyes wide.

I want to kiss her.

I won't. Not today. Definitely not after what she's been through. But I want to own that pouty mouth. Want to taste those lips, shove my tongue deep and make her take it the way I want to give it.

But with her fucking consent.

My fists tighten thinking about Brumgard again. I'm already regretting not killing him.

"Let me off, let me off," Pink wails and I slap the bars to slow them down, then grab one and jog around with it until it stops. Bailey holds her belly like she's going to barf.

"Sorry. Too much?" I put a hand on her back. I literally feel the shiver run through her. Or maybe that was the sparks that came through in my hand.

I'm suddenly acutely aware of everything Bailey: her hitched breath, her cinnamon and honey scent, the strands of hair flying across her face.

I smooth them back and she stares up at me. "Why are you being so nice to me?"

I crash into the vulnerability in her eyes. Something shifts in my chest. Guilt, perhaps—I don't know. Maybe something else. I drown in her warm brown gaze, studying the golden and green flecks. I have to look away. "I don't know."

It's an honest answer. I really can't explain why I flipped from tormentor to protector in the blink of an eye. And I know it won't last. I'll take her home and tomorrow we'll wake up enemies again.

And I'm not going to admit that's part of why I haven't taken her home yet.

I shove my hands in my pockets to keep from reaching for her. "Listen. What happened back at the school"—I pull one hand out and jerk my thumb in the direction of Wolf Ridge High—"is your thing. I won't talk about it unless you ask me. Whatever you want to do with it is fine."

"Thanks." I hear relief in her voice, and I know I said the right thing.

"I'll be a witness if you want to press charges. If you want to go to Mr. Olsen and get him fired. Otherwise, I won't tell a soul. If you don't want your shit dragged all over this town, I get that, too."

Her eyes get wet again. When a tear escapes and hops down her cheek, I brush it away with my fingertips.

"I don't want you to feel like you have to hide it, though. You may think you're a victim, but you hold all the power now."

Her energy quiets. I swear I feel her shaking off the victim cloak right there. "What do you mean?"

I unleash a wicked smile. "I mean," I say slowly, the glory of revenge gleaming bright for me. "If you don't go to the authorities, you own Brumgard. You can ditch every class for the rest of the year and insist he give you an A and he'll do it. Make him write your college essays for you. Make him nominate you for end of the year awards."

She rolls her eyes. "That's what you would do if you were me."

My smile grows bigger. "Definitely. And it's what you should do. Of course, it'll suck for me when you're not in class to help me with the quizzes. I never said thanks, by the way."

Her eyebrows pop and then she blushes.

I *fucking love* when she blushes. I flip back into tormentor mode as quickly as that. I reach out and finger her earlobe, stroking the little flap softly.

She jerks her head away. "Fuck you, Cole."

"Oh, I'm planning on it, Pink," I say in a low and seductive voice.

Blushing deeper, she shoves at my chest and turns to walk swiftly back to the truck.

Chuckling, I follow.

She hops in her seat and crosses her arms over her chest. As if that will protect her from me.

I get in the truck and start it up. "I will say this, though, Pink."

She turns at the business-like tone of my voice. I like that she already gets me—when I'm serious, when I'm dicking with her.

"One word to any parent in Wolf Ridge and a posse of dads will go down to the school and literally kick Brumgard's ass and then get him thrown out of the school. I guarantee you that. So I'm just saying—it's on the table, if that's what you want."

I speak with total certainty. Bailey may not be pack, but she's a kid at our school. Every father in Wolf Ridge would realize it could've been their pup who was assaulted, and they would be out for blood. Brumgard may be a human, but they'd make him pay, anyway. And I guarantee Alpha Green would turn a blind eye to every pack rule that goes against.

Bailey rubs her tattoo—the one I want to know more about. "Okay, good to know."

"You want me to get it rolling? I'll do it."

"No." She shakes her head, still staring at her ink. "I don't know. I just need some time to think things over. I just want to keep it between us for now." She shrugs.

"Okay." I pull back out onto the dirt road. "You hold the power," I remind her.

But then I wish I hadn't, because the look she sends me —the gratitude there—does all kinds of fucked up things with my head.

CHAPTER 5

 *ailey*

COLE PULLS UP in the alley behind our houses instead of on the street. I'm about to ask him why, when I catch sight of his dad standing on the back porch, staring us down with murder in his eyes.

"Fuck," Cole mutters.

His dad looks off. Sweaty. Red-faced. Disheveled clothing and hair. He's holding the customary beer bottle in his hand.

Chills run down my arms. Is Cole going to be in trouble for coming home with me—the enemy's daughter —in his truck?

"Get out, Pink," he says tightly, not taking his eyes off his dad.

I don't wait. I dive out of the truck and jog around the far side of my house away from Cole's house to the front door. Even though it feels like I severed a limb and left it in Cole's cab, I'm almost grateful for the sudden parting. It saves me the awkwardness of figuring out what to say and trying to decipher what things will be like between us tomorrow.

My mom isn't home yet which isn't a surprise. She works late every night, sometimes until eight, trying to get the regulatory situation cleaned up at the brewery.

I pull out a box of mac 'n cheese and put a pot of water on to boil.

And that's when I hear it. Even though I know immediately who it is, I try to tell myself it won't be them—not Cole and his dad yelling outside. Because I last saw them in back, and these voices are coming from the front.

I open the front door and choke on my own spit.

It's a full-on brawl on the sidewalk. No, not a brawl. A one-sided fight with Cole's dad on top and Cole covering his head and face and dodging the blows. Behind them, Casey screams, "Stop it!" from the flagstone steps. "Dad! Stop it!"

I scream too. I don't know what I say—maybe Cole's name.

His dad looks up, pauses to glare. It gives Cole time to scramble out from under him.

"Get back in your house," his dad snarls at me. He slurs slightly, definitely drunk.

"Cole," I rasp, my throat raw from screaming.

"Get in the house, Pink." Cole spits a mouthful of blood out on the ground. His dad lunges again, but Cole dodges him.

I run back inside for my phone, then come back out,

my thumb hovering over the keys to call 911. But I can't bring myself to dial.

I refused to go into the sheriff's today. I didn't want my story spread far and wide.

Maybe Cole doesn't want his home life problems public, either.

"Dad, stop!" Casey cries, hovering a few feet away. "Bring it back inside."

Her dad takes Cole to the ground again, landing several bone-crunching punches that make me want to puke.

A neighbor shows up, the guy who lives across the street, I think. "That's enough, Jerry," he shouts, jumping into the fray and grabbing Cole's dad's shoulder. Jerry shakes him off. "John, help me get him off!" he shouts to another neighbor who's come out to witness the horrific scene.

"You get inside," he tells me. "You're only making it worse."

The words rattle inside my skull.

This *is* about me. And I'm making it worse. I turn and run to my house.

I don't realize I'm sobbing until I'm inside, watching from the cracked door as the two neighbors drag Jerry off Cole.

"This can't go on, Jerry," the neighbor says. He finally succeeds in getting Jerry away and the drunk man shakes himself off and stalks past his flinching daughter to go inside.

The neighbor helps Cole to his feet.

I creep back out. I don't know what I think I can do.

All I know is I can't just stay inside my house when Cole is suffering outside.

"Might be time to fight back, son," the neighbor says to Cole in a low voice.

Cole throws the neighbor's hand off his shoulder. "Go fuck yourself, Lon."

"You watch your language, boy." The neighbor's tone turns sharp, but Cole gives it right back, crowding into his space without raising a fist. Bowing up, pushing his chest against the older man's chest and eyeballing him like he wants to fight.

The neighbor, Lon, puts a hand on Cole's chest and shoves him back. "I'm not your enemy."

Blood drips down Cole's nose and mouth, coating his lips. "Neither is he." He jerks his head toward the house.

The neighbor shakes his head, turning away. "I know it." There's defeat in his tone and the slump of his shoulders.

There's rage in Cole's. He stalks up his steps and slams the front door, the sound reverberating all the way down to my soul.

I go inside, shutting my door as quietly as I can. And when the tears start falling, I try not to make a sound. And when I can't hold in the sobs shaking through me so hard my bones ache, I cover my mouth and cry some more. I cry for the boy next door. I cry for the boy who hates me so he doesn't have to hate his father.

CHAPTER 6

ole

IT'S past midnight when I wake up. My window's open,
moonlight streaming in.

That wasn't what woke me, though.

It wasn't the pain of the beating, either. That's already
half-healed. By tomorrow it will be nothing.

That's the thing about wolf discipline. It's more about
dominance and humiliation than actual pain. Casey and I
aren't in real danger.

But that doesn't mean the shit doesn't hurt.

I rub the stubble on my chin and blink into the darkness. There's a tug on my wolf, pulling me to the window.
And I know exactly what I'm going to see when I look out.

Even so, my heart stutters.

The little human is standing outside. Standing underneath my window, looking up.

Like she's waiting for me and she knew I'd come. Prickles run across my skin.

She's in the same dress she wore today—another short one, blue and white stripes. She lost the Converse, though. She's barefooted on the crushed granite. Which must hurt her tender human feet.

I'm in gym shorts. I pull on a black tank top as I stare down at her.

She's standing there like a fucking tribute. A virginal offering.

She must really feel guilty.

I shove the window open and pop the screen out. It's not the first time I've climbed out this window, but I try not to make it look too easy when I scale across the patio overhang and drop to the gravel in front of her. "Hey."

She's crying. Silent tears that streak down her pale cheeks. I wonder if she ever stopped. If she's been leaking those salty tears since she saw the ugliness that is my dad shit-faced. The scent of her tears does something to me. Makes me itchy and raw, with the need to smash things with my fists.

"Stop it." I sound menacing. I'm not sorry. She silently called me out here. She's gonna get what she gets. I advance on her like a fucking predator.

She backs up. She must sense how dangerous I am right now. How unhinged.

"Was it because of me?"

Of course it was because of her. But I'm not going to say that. That shit isn't her fault.

Instead, I growl, "Stop crying for me."

Her big brown eyes are wide. I wonder how well she can see me in the dark. Not nearly as well as I can see her.

"*Stop it,*" I command. "I'm the one who got the beatdown."

"Cole." It's a broken syllable. Small and quavering. So much emotion packed into one sound. Apology. Pleading. Desperation, even.

My control snaps. I snatch her face up to mine with a hand behind her head and devour her mouth. It tastes like all the emotion I heard.

Except more.

I savor gratitude and soft, supple generosity. Pent up anger. Grief.

Desire.

I scoop my forearm under her ass to pick her up and slam her back against the tan stucco of her house.

She opens her lips for me, lets me in. It's not how I imagined it.

It's better.

More raw. Sweeter, even though I'm fucking brutal with my attack. Her lips twist over mine with the same intensity, her nails claw into my bare shoulders. I shove the bulge of my cock in the cradle of her legs, even though I know it will probably scare the shit out of her.

I keep kissing, fucking her mouth with my tongue. The cut on my lip reopens and blood seeps into the kiss.

Good.

Let her taste how I bled for her. I'm going to make her bleed too. Need to taste it on my lips. Have it smeared over my cock. Maybe not tonight, but I'm going to get it.

I shift to grab her ass with both hands, squeeze and

knead those firm globes. I catch skin with one of my fingers and lust ratchets higher. I thrust against the thin fabric of her panties, rubbing my cock over her clit.

The sweet smell of her arousal fills my nostrils.

She wants it.

I break the kiss and drop my head into the crook of her neck, biting down on the flesh there. I stay like that, my body mashed up against hers, a slow grind at the juncture of her thighs. We're both breathing hard.

I need to put her down. Send her back inside.

I know she's not ready for all the things I want to do to her. And my control is shit right now.

Need sky high.

But instead of letting her go, I go dirty. I let my fingertips trace along the seam of her ass. She gasps and squirms, her inner thighs tightening around my waist as she tries unsuccessfully to squeeze her cheeks together.

Yeah, baby. I'll take that too, eventually.

But I'm not that big an asshole tonight.

"You'd better get back inside, Pink," I breathe against her neck. My lips brush her skin. She tastes so fucking good.

She whimpers softly but doesn't move.

I realize I'm torturing her. Her body's turned on, revved up to go and now I'm going to send her in.

It's a torture to me, too, but I can take it. A teen wolf my age has already been fighting this shit for at least four years. At least the moon's not full.

I give her another hard kiss. I go in boldly for her asshole this time, rubbing firmly as I thrust my cock against her wet panties and suck on her lips.

She bucks a little.

Fates, did she just orgasm?

I think she might have.

That nearly tears me apart.

Like my eye color probably changed and I have to stop the very wolf-sounding snarl from coming out of my throat.

I force myself to set her feet down, but all the while I'm stroking her ass, squeezing, kneading, loving it up with both palms. All the while, I'm kissing the hell out of her.

She tastes so fucking good.

"Get inside," I growl. My voice sounds three octaves lower than usual, and rough as sandpaper. "Before I fucking ruin you."

She's trembling. Her whole body's shaking, and she has to hang on to my forearms to stand on her feet.

"How do you know I'm not already ruined?" She sounds breathless.

I let out a mirthless laugh and lean my forehead against hers. "I know. Because I've already decided I'm gonna be the guy to destroy you. Now get inside."

She doesn't move. Her breaths are short. Her body still trembles. "You're still holding on to me," she says.

Ah. So I am. My hands are still cupping her delicious ass. I still have her trapped between my body and the house.

I ease back, biting back the groan of disappointment at losing contact.

And then, because I can, because I want to, I catch her

wrists, turn her slowly to face the house and press her palms flat against the rough texture of the stucco.

She doesn't expect the sharp smack of my hand on her ass. Her gasp is part yelp. I squeeze and rub away the sting, and lean close to put my lips beside her ear. "Don't get smart with me, Pink."

The fresh scent of her arousal greets me, making it pure torture to let her go.

I release her wrists but slap her ass one more time. "Get inside." My palm tingles with the impact. I'm sure her ass will for more than a few minutes.

Good. I want her to feel me.

Feel the pain I choose to give her.

And the pleasure.

I'm going to give it to her every way I desire.

And she's going to love taking it.

CHAPTER 7

ailey

I GO through my first few classes the next day in a stupor. I should be exhausted but I'm not. I'm keyed up. Antsy. A little sick. Nervous. Confused. And underneath it all simmers excitement I'm afraid to even acknowledge or let out.

Cole Muchmore kissed me.

I mean really and thoroughly kissed me.

And it felt like he doused me in lighter fluid and sparked a match, because my whole body is still on fire. My skin is branded everywhere he touched.

I want more of it—so much more.

And even though he promised more—in the most threatening kind of way—I have no idea what to expect from him today, and that terrifies me.

And even more pressing, I have to figure out what I'm

going to do about the Brumgard situation. Last night turned into such a cluster, I couldn't think straight.

I still don't want to run to the principal or the police. I'm already a leper at this school. I don't need this kind of stigma, too.

The idea that appeals to me most is just avoiding the whole thing. Not returning to class. Blackmailing him for an A and my recommendations.

No, that's a lie. Ditching class and getting out of work doesn't excite me.

What I'd prefer is a teacher with integrity, who would've actually worked with me on starting a newspaper. But that's an impossibility. There will be no Wolf Ridge High newspaper. No chance to get a byline and build my clips for my college paper. No opportunity to make a difference and leave my mark on this school.

I fantasize about walking into class with my head held high. Brumgard should be the one who wants to hide, not me. But when the time comes for class, I feel like puking. I stand at my locker, even though I don't need any books. I'm hiding there.

Okay, if I'm completely honest with myself, I'd admit I'm waiting for Cole to appear. To tell me what to do. Or be my shield. Or just offer some kind of support.

But that's stupid.

He may have kissed me last night, but it doesn't mean he plans to continue anything. Yesterday could've been a one-off. Twenty-four hours of crazytown where the shit hit the fan for each of us and we stood by each other.

The halls start clearing out, kids heading into their

classes before the late bell rings. I suck in my breath and close my locker.

Cole's coming down the hall surrounded by his pack of friends. I expect to see his face bruised and swollen, but it's not. In fact, I can hardly tell anything happened last night. I guess he wasn't hurt as bad as I thought. He's listening to a friend now and doesn't look at me.

And that settles it.

No way in hell I am going in that classroom. I'm way too raw and exposed. I can't pretend everything's okay when it's so *not*.

As the group of alpha-holes pass, I duck my head, looking at the ground. Only at the last minute, I can't help myself. I look over at Cole again.

He looks too. At the same moment.

Nothing changes on his face; his cocky smirk is firmly in place. If I blinked I would miss it, but he winks at me.

And just like that, the world is right again.

No, not right. But so much better. I can breathe. I can think clearly.

I savor that wink—a shared secret between us—and I keep walking, straight out the door to the little patch of shady trees Rayne showed me.

Like Cole said, I don't have to go to class if I don't want to.

In fact, I could probably still work on this newspaper project as my own personal independent study. It can be part of my blackmail. Brumgard has to publish whatever I put together.

Feeling much better, I pull out a notebook and try to

recall the list of potential articles I brainstormed on his whiteboard yesterday.

Cole was right. I do hold the power.

And I intend to use it.

COLE

BRUMGARD'S NOSE is swollen three times the normal size and both his eyes are black. I hear him tell a kid he had a door opened on his face as I'm walking in.

He's gonna have a door shut on his dick if he so much as mentions Bailey's name.

Bailey had that same pale pinched look on her face before class that she had yesterday—fates, was it only yesterday? Feels like weeks ago. It makes me want to punch Brumgard all over again.

But I'm glad she didn't come to class.

She shouldn't ever have to sit through another Brumgard lecture.

And I will personally make sure he writes her the best goddamn college recommendations ever created. I saunter over to his desk and read the papers on it until the bell rings and he comes over. Anger and fear flicker over his face at the sight of me.

I lean in close, taking advantage of the shuffling in the room as kids sit down to say what I have to say. Fates know, most of the class has shifter hearing and Brumgard doesn't, so speaking in a low voice isn't going to work if anyone's listening.

I scent his fear.

"Bailey's not coming to class, but you're not going to mark her absent," I murmur.

I don't wait for his answer. I know he's going to do what I ask.

He has to. I have so much fucking leverage over this man right now, it's crazy.

I head to my seat where I plop down, fold my arms over my chest and glower at him as he starts the lecture.

Every time he looks my way, he loses his cool and stammers, forgetting what he's saying. I glory over the sweat dripping down his forehead.

He'd better sweat it.

He'd better sweat me for the rest of his goddamn life.

Fucking pervert.

Austin nudges me and lifts his chin toward Pink's empty chair. "Where's the *human*?" He mouths the last word, even though most students at Wolf Ridge are pack. There are some unsuspecting humans who go here—probably less than twenty percent, and all socially marginalized like Bailey. For faculty, we're not quite so homogenous. More than half of them are human. Alpha Green thinks it's important for integration that we learn to blend into the American culture without humans knowing what we are.

I scowl because I'm not going to tell him where Bailey is, and also, I'm still pissed about the reason for her absence.

He raises his brows.

I force my scowl away and shrug my shoulders like I don't give a shit.

I doubt I succeed, especially since Austin knows me better than anyone, but Bailey's story isn't mine to tell.

I think about Pink. What I know about her now. The scent of her tears. The taste of her skin. The way her ass feels in my hands.

She gave me her vulnerability yesterday.

Robbed me of mine.

I want to still hate her. Especially after what she witnessed in front of my house.

But I don't.

We're in this together now. We've shared each other's nightmares.

And when I took from her, she gave.

Let me kiss those swollen lips. Let me dry fuck her against a wall.

I woke up this morning thinking I needed space. Get this human off my mind before she gets even further under my skin.

I planned on pretending she didn't exist when I saw her today. Reasoned she probably needed the space, too.

But it didn't last. The minute I saw her, I tumbled back to where we were last night, standing between our houses under the moon.

And now I'm already itchy for more.

I need to finish this thing I started with her.

I can't stop until I fully own Bailey Sanchez. Until she's given me every secret, every lie, every tear. I crave the moment I take everything from her.

Crave it like my next breath.

~

BAILEY

AFTER SCHOOL I hang by my locker. It's stupid, I'm going to miss the bus if I don't hurry, but I want to see Cole. Want to talk to him again. Find out what happened in journalism class. Tell him what I decided.

I wait until I'm going to have to run to catch the bus, and then I give up, shut my locker and head down the emptying halls. When I round the bend into the junior and sophomore hallway, my steps falter.

Casey Muchmore is at her locker with a group of friends and when she sees me, she looks like she wants to draw blood. She says something to her friends and leaves them, walking right toward me. The friends stay at the lockers, but watch in sick fascination.

I tell myself not to be afraid of an underclassman, but it doesn't work. After the way Rayne was really scared Adriana would hurt me, I'm not sure what to expect from the girls at Wolf Ridge. Sounds like they're as likely to get into fights as the boys, which scares the crap out of me.

I want to pretend I don't see her and walk on by, but it's not the right thing to do. I saw something ugly in her family last night, and if she's pissed, it's probably partially because she's ashamed of what I saw. So I'm not going to blow her off, as much as I'd like to.

Turns out I couldn't have anyway. She plants her body directly in my path so I have to stop. Her posture is aggressive: hands on her hips, chin up, jaw set.

"I'm sorry if I caused a problem," I say immediately, even though it's not my fault their dad is an abusive asshole.

Her nostrils flare. "You did," she says. "You stay away from my brother or I'm going to kick your ass. He hates you, anyway."

She aimed to hurt and she succeeds. Whether it's one hundred percent true, or only partially true—her barb pierces because I know she's right.

Cole does hate me.

There was violence in his kisses last night. Pent up anger, blame, resentment.

But they were still kisses.

Kisses that incited a wildfire inside me. That kept me up all night touching myself, trying to get relief from the pulsing in my core.

And I didn't sleep before we met outside his window, either. I crawled into bed with my mom when she got home, and I told her about Cole and we both had a long cry over the situation next door.

I didn't tell her about Brumgard. I'm still not ready to open that subject with anyone but Cole.

Casey's gaze shifts from my face to the end of the hallway behind me and she grimaces.

I turn to see Cole and his buddies gathered, Cole staring down the hall at us.

Casey points a finger in my face. "I'm serious. You stay away." She starts backing up.

"Stay out of it, Case." Cole's voice is low and his tread silent as he approaches us without his friends.

Casey stops her retreat and squares off to him.

"Pink is my problem, not yours."

His problem.

I have the urge to just walk away. Escape this conversation about me between the siblings. Leave before the knife twists deeper.

But my feet don't obey my brain. They stay planted right where they are. Needing to be near Cole.

"Interfere and I'll make you sorry, little sister," Cole warns.

I am somewhat relieved to see that despite the threat, she doesn't appear afraid. Their dad may be abusive, but the siblings must be tight. Casey just watches him like she's trying to decipher his intentions.

Or maybe that's just my projection, since I'm somewhat desperate to know them, myself.

After a few beats, she shakes her head like she's disgusted with both of us and walks away.

Cole catches her arm and rubberbands her back. "Leave it, Case. Stay out of my business."

She shoots a glance in my direction, then back at Cole. "It affects both of us," she says tightly.

My gut twists. She's right. If Cole spending time with me enrages their father, it would affect both kids.

Cole shakes his head. "Nothing else will happen. Now *leave it.*"

Her face colors slightly. "Fine." She turns and flounces off, back to her friends while I stand there with my own cheeks burning.

"I told Brumgard not to mark you absent," Cole murmurs as soon as she's gone. "Everything's cool."

My relief is not around being marked absent or present,

it's knowing Cole still has my back. My shoulders relax. I tuck my hair behind one ear and duck my head, suddenly shy. "Thank you."

But of course, Cole can't ever just be kind. "I don't want your thanks," he sneers, pinching my chin to lift it.

I flinch under his dark gaze.

The hatred is still there.

I don't know why my core tightens and my toes curl when he looks at me like that. There must be something wrong with me. Why would a girl get turned on by a hate-glare?

He pulls his phone out of his back pocket and thrusts it at me. It's an old model and the screen is broken. "Text yourself," he commands.

I'm not dumb enough this time to get excited. He wants my number—so what? It might just be to communicate about Brumgard so he doesn't have to stop and talk to me in person again.

I text myself the word "text" because I can't think of anything clever and hand the phone back.

I turn to go but he grabs my arm, just like he did his sister's. "Hey."

I turn to face him with my own glare this time.

His brow furrows and he lowers his face to mine. "Don't ever come out of your house when my dad is there," he orders. "Don't let him see you. Got it?"

My stomach churns and all the angst over he-likes-me, he-likes-me-not evaporates. This is so much bigger than teenage drama. Cole lives a nightmare every day.

"I don't care what you hear, you stay inside," he warns.

I can't help it. Tears pop into my eyes.

"Don't," he snarls. He slams his fist into the lockers behind my head, denting them. "Don't fucking cry for me."

I drop my eyes because I'm crying more now and the tears freefall to my Day of the Dead skull Chucks.

And then it happens again. His hands are on my ass and my nape, his lips are over mine. It's punishment.

Reward.

Connection.

I don't know what it is, but I want every bit of it as badly as he does. His lips tear over mine, palm squeezes my ass hard enough to leave fingermarks. His other hand controls my head, holding it for the onslaught of lips and tongue, lifting my face toward him.

My whole body trembles for him.

I have no sense of time, but it goes on for an eternity. The blink of an eye. I don't know.

Then he suddenly pulls away, releases all of me and steps back. A moment later, a teacher rounds the bend and stops, hands on her prim hips, "Aren't you supposed to be at practice, Cole?"

Did he hear her coming? That doesn't make sense. But he cocks his head like he's listening to something and then he grins. "You missed your bus, Pink. Looks like you'll have to walk."

Asshole.

Is he taunting me? Did he do that on purpose? Make me think he likes me, make me tremble for him, just to make my life hell?

I scowl and turn on my heel, hurrying down the hallway to hide my flaming face.

"Pink."

I don't stop.

"I want you at my game Friday."

I hold up my hand with my middle finger extended, still not stopping or looking back.

I hear his chuckle as I exit the building.

Fuck him. I'm sure he plans to humiliate me in some new way. I would be stupid to comply.

COLE

I SAUNTER DOWN THE HALL, past Ms. Eller, the French teacher and a member of the pack. She'd probably tell Alpha Green I'm screwing around with a human. Or maybe she was trying to save Pink from my torment. That's a good possibility too. I'm not known for my kindness around here.

I didn't mean to kiss Bailey again. But those tears. I don't know what it is. The fact that this little slip of a human sheds tears for me—the guy who's been nothing but an asshole to her. It does something to me.

She tasted like strawberries and melon today. And her sweet honey and cookies scent, which for some reason, my wolf is coming to love.

It's on me now—on my palms, on my face. The front of my shirt from when I pressed up against her. I bring my palm to my nose and inhale deeply.

Pleasure rushes through me.

Pleasure and need. I sprouted a chub the moment I touched her and my cock aches now for release. And it's not like I have time to beat one off in the locker bathroom before practice. I'm already late enough that Coach is going to make me run laps.

In the locker room, I yank off my t-shirt and bring it to my nose. Fuck it smells good. I shove the shirt down in my bag to jack off with later.

Maybe Bailey will leave her shade open while she changes tonight. I caught a glimpse of her boobs once when she first moved in. She came in from the bathroom in a towel and let it drop before she realized the shades were open. I laughed my ass off as she dived for the shades with one hand trying to cover those pert little nipples.

Maybe I'll order her to leave it open and see if she complies. She just might. I felt the way she trembled when I kissed her. She opened to me again, like she's been waiting for me to claim her. Even though she knows I'm the worst thing for her.

I'm her weakness.

Just like she's mine.

CHAPTER 8

 *ailey*

"I THINK WE NEED A GOSSIP COLUMN." Rayne taps her pen against the glass of my kitchen table.

I haven't told her what happened. It's not that I don't think she'd give me the support of a friend, it's more that I don't have my own head wrapped around it. And Cole's story is tied up with mine and it doesn't feel right sharing that part of it.

I did tell her I'm going to start a school newspaper and offered her an editor position, which she accepted.

Hence, the big editorial meeting at my house after school.

We haven't come up with any good ideas, but I don't mind. It's nice to have company.

It's been a long time.

"This town definitely doesn't need any more gossip.

But we could do feature articles. Highlight some of the less popular, lesser-known students and their talents."

Rayne's mouth falls open like I said something shocking. "Wow. We could do that?"

"Why not? Everyone probably already knows everything about Adriana, the sweet, cuddly homecoming queen who wants to kill me." Rayne laughs. "But do they know… I don't know, about some secret talent of some shy girl no one talks to?"

A scheming glow comes over Rayne's face. "I want to write these. I know exactly who to highlight."

"You do?"

"Yep. And I'm starting with you. There are a lot of kids like you who people sort of refuse to get to know."

"Kids like me?" I don't know why I press. I know she already said my rejection wasn't racially motivated, but I still feel like there's something.

When Rayne drops her eyes to her notebook too quickly, that feeling is reinforced. "I mean kids who aren't originally from Wolf Ridge or don't live up here, but just go to school for the sports or whatever. Outsiders."

Something doesn't ring quite true in her words, even though I can't argue with what she's saying. I just keep thinking it's something else. Like maybe Brumgard was right; they are all in some kind of closed cult.

I don't like the prickle that runs over my arms and the stone that sits at the bottom of my stomach.

Does Wolf Ridge have a secret? If so, what the hell is it?

~

COLE

It's a home game and the stadiums are full. I keep scanning them, looking for Pink.

I told her to come.

She flipped me off.

Doesn't mean she won't be here, though. And if she is, I'm counting it as a huge fucking victory. If she is, I'm going to make sure I get my hands on her again. All over her.

I texted her one word the night she gave me her phone. "Me."

I wanted her to have my number in case she wants to communicate about the Brumgard thing. At least that's what I told myself.

I wasn't entirely surprised when she didn't respond.

I've been a dick to her and she doesn't trust me, even though she wants to.

I can't decide if *I* want her to.

All I know is that she's my obsession. I look down at her window every night with my cock in my hand, thinking of the things I want to do to her.

It's the fourth quarter of the game before I spot the white-blonde mop of hair that belongs to the pack runt, Rayne. And next to her, the hot nerdy human.

My hot human.

She may not know she's mine yet, but she'll learn. Her little friend Rayne already knows.

What I'm going to do with her, I don't know. All I

know is that she's mine to torment. Mine to punish. Mine to… protect.

Yeah, she's definitely under my protection.

When I saw Casey threatening her, I had to work to keep my temper in check. To act human and not show a little teeth in staking my claim. My jurisdiction. Nobody makes threats to the bookish hottie but me.

No one touches her.

So I glory in the fact that she's here. I told her to come and she came. It's a total victory, and one I'm going to celebrate tonight. With her, if I can figure out how to lose my buddies without them knowing what I'm up to.

I'm so happy I get too handy with the ball. I throw it down the entire field for a touchdown before I realize what I'm doing.

The stadium shakes with the roar of approval from the crowd, but I can see Coach Jamison staring me down from the sidelines. Oh sure, he pumps his fist in the air like he's supposed to, but his posture is irritation, not victory.

Our defense holds back for the next snap of the ball and we let them get a field goal in.

I'm hardly paying attention. All I can think about is getting between the thighs of that infuriating, beautiful human up in the stands.

I play it cool. Fumble the ball to make up for my earlier zeal. Steal it back at the last minute for another touchdown. Strut around the field like the stud I am, soaking up the cheers of the fans. My dad's out there, too.

That used to mean something different to me. I used to do my very best, knowing we'd sit down after the game and pick the whole thing apart. Every move I made, every player on each team. Now he comes but he's drinking. He yells too loud, embarrasses me. After the game he hardly remembers what happened.

But I'm always acutely aware of his presence. Still wanting to please him even though he doesn't care like he used to.

We win the game without overly trouncing the opposing team—which is always our goal—and pat each other's asses as we walk into the locker room. I go straight to my locker and grab my phone.

You came, I text Pink.

I'm satisfied when she answers immediately. *Only for Rayne.*

I grin. *Bullshit. You came because I asked.*

That wasn't asking. That was alpha-hole ordering.

My smile gets wider at her use of a very Wolf Ridge term. *Babygirl, you don't know the first thing about alpha-holes. But I'd be happy to show you.*

Giving Pink shit was always the goal, but where it came from a dark bitterness before, it's turning into something else. The need to get under her skin is just as intense, but the way it makes me feel is different.

Definitely alpha, she's right.

Nah, I'm good, she texts back.

"What are you smiling at?" Bo asks, looking over my shoulder.

I hide my phone from his view. "Nunya."

Austin and Wilde look over like they know exactly who I'm texting.

Fuckers.

I look back at my screen, trying to come up with a

plan. I can't be seen with her, not by my dad. Not by my friends. Not by any pack member, which is pretty much most everyone in the fucking stadium. *Meet me in the Dairy Queen parking lot in a half hour.*

I stare at my screen but she doesn't answer.

That makes me smile, too. I like it when she gives it back to me. I like her spunk. Her smart mouth.

Those earnest tears.

My cock twitches and I toss my phone back in my locker before I get a full-on boner in front of the whole team. I hope she shows up tonight. She'd better, because if she doesn't, I'm gonna make sure I find her, and there will be hell to pay.

And that makes me smile, too.

Not even the ass-chewing Coach Jamison gives me for throwing the ball too far brings me down.

BAILEY

THERE'S no way in hell I'm going to go meet Cole Muchmore in the Dairy Queen parking lot. I don't know why my stomach is in twists and flutters thinking about it.

Rayne and I walk around the block to where it's not quite so embarrassing to be picked up by my mom who pulls up in her Corolla, still wearing work clothes.

"Hi, girls, how was it?" she asks overly brightly. She's thrilled I made a friend.

"Okay." I slide into the front seat and Rayne climbs in the back. "Are you just getting off work?"

"Yes. I decided to work late since I knew I was picking you two up. Tell your mom thanks for driving you over." My mom looks over her shoulder and smiles at Rayne.

I fiddle with the radio, switching stations until it lands on an 80s song my mom likes by the Cure, *Friday I'm in Love*.

My mom cranks it..

When we get to Rayne's house, I hop out to give her a hug.

"Be careful," she murmurs in my ear.

I pull away. "What do you mean?"

"You're going to meet Cole. Just be careful."

I hadn't shown her the texts—she must've peeked. I'm not pissed, though. It's nice that she has my back. "I'm not going," I say quickly.

"You're thinking about it."

I shake my head. "You're wiser than your age, you know that?"

"That's what happens when you're the runt. Plenty of time to observe because you're always left out."

I blink, gutted to hear her voice what I'd only sensed about her social life. "Fuck. I'm sorry."

She shrugs and lifts her chin toward the car. "Go. Your mom's waiting. Just be careful. Gird your loins." She grins.

"Gird my loins." I snort. "I think that's my new favorite saying."

"As it should be. Let me know how it goes."

"I'm not going," I insist, but she just mumbles, "Yeah right" as she heads to her door.

Twenty minutes later, I tell my mom I'm going to run to Dairy Queen. It's a sign of how broken I've been that she's delighted rather than shocked. "Are you taking the car?" The hope in her voice is too obvious.

"No, I'll walk."

Now she frowns. "That sounds like a bad idea."

"Wolf Ridge has to be the safest area in all of northern Phoenix. Everyone knows each other around here. What could happen?"

Her eyes narrow. "Why didn't you ask to stop there when we passed it on the way? Are you meeting someone?"

I tuck the pink chunk of my hair behind my ear. "Maybe. Yeah. I don't know. I'm a little late now."

"Well, let me drive you back there."

"No," I say quickly. Eighteen-year-olds shouldn't be getting rides from their moms. It's just stupid. "I'll see you later—bye!" I run out before we can discuss it any further.

As I walk down the street, the conversations in my head run marathon loops. It's a bad idea to meet Cole Muchmore. He's an alpha-hole looking to score. He wants to use me. No, it's worse than that. He's still out to punish me because of my mom. And his dad. And what I saw and know about his home life.

But he's also the guy who punched Mr. Brumgard in the face. And took me to the abandoned playground. And made sure it was okay for me to skip class.

And hasn't told anyone about what happened, as far as I know.

So I can't just write him off. And then there's our very strong physical attraction.

I hit puberty at twelve. Got my period and breasts and hips. Fooled around with some kids at parties. But my sexual awakening didn't happen until I met Cole Muchmore.

It's like my body comes alive around him. I only just realized I'm a sexual being with needs and desires. And those desires could be fulfilled by my hot, dickwad neighbor.

So, yeah. It's a bad idea, but I'm still going.

I'm testing fate, because I stalled long enough that I'm now late. He may just assume I'm not coming and leave. And that would be fine.

I take the side streets there. It's been an hour since Cole's text, and when I arrive, the Dairy Queen is closed. The parking lot is empty.

Except for the old classic Ford truck parked in the back corner.

My heart starts hammering. He waited an extra thirty minutes to see if I'd show.

Cole slides out of the driver's side, his moves languid and graceful for such a big guy. Anger radiates from him.

I falter, then stop.

Cole stops, too, leaving three feet of space between us, like he sees I'm scared and doesn't want to freak me out. "You walked here from home? Christ, Pink, are you nuts? You do know it's eleven at night, right?"

My brows shoot up in surprise. He's mad I walked? Not that I'm late or that he thought I wasn't coming?

"I don't drive," I tell him.

He rolls his eyes. "Yeah, I know." Now he steps in closer, which is exactly where my body wants him to be. He tilts his head to the side. "Why is that, Pink?"

I shake my head. I'm definitely not discussing it with him. I must've unconsciously rubbed my tattoo because he grabs my wrists to stop the movement and examines the Catrina skull. In full Day of the Dead tradition, it's decorated with flowers for eyes, and vines and leaves. A wreath of roses around the head.

"Because of this?" Cole demands.

Shock ripples through me at his guess. I try to pull my hands away, but he holds me fast. "Who was Catrina? She died in a car accident?"

I look up to the stars to keep the tears that filled my eyes from falling. I suddenly can't breathe at all. My throat's too tight. Too choked with sharp edges of grief that scrape and burn.

"Fuck, Pink." Cole sounds shocked, like whatever he sees on my face unnerves him. He cradles one side of my head and yanks me against his hard form. My cheek hits his muscled chest, and I draw in a horrible, loud sobbing breath. "Fuck," he mutters again. "Who was she?"

I haven't talked about it. Everyone at my old school knew the story. They were all careful not to bring it up around me.

Now it all comes out at once. The crushing guilt. The trauma. The agony of loss.

"My best friend," I croak against his t-shirt. My tears are already soaking the soft cotton. "I killed her."

"Fuck." His arms tighten around me.

I sob it out, ugly shaking, heaving cries against the chest of my enemy.

As fast as it came on, it stops. Like I just had this tidal wave in me that needed to come out, and then the waters stilled.

I stop shaking and lift my head. I suddenly want to tell him. Want to say the words out loud and have them witnessed. "I was driving and the road was icy. We spun out of control and smashed into a guard rail. A piece of metal came through the windshield and punctured her skull. One minute we were joking about her ability to make popcorn, the next minute she was gone. Not just gone, a scene that plays in my nightmares. My best friend, eyes unblinking and the blood. So much blood."

I sense Cole's shock, but his face shows nothing. I'm grateful not to see sympathy or horror. Just grim acknowledgment.

"So now you don't drive." It's a statement.

I nod.

"Because you're scared or to punish yourself?"

Hmm. Good question. I'm grateful for the chance to untangle the hulking mess that's been my past. "Both, I guess."

He shakes his head like it's the wrong answer. "You're driving," he says firmly, like I'm in big trouble and he's laying down the law. He takes my elbow firmly and tugs me toward the driver side of his truck.

I resist, but he's too strong and sure. He pushes me up against the door, pressing his body against mine from behind. His cock is hard, but this doesn't feel totally sexual. It's something more. He wraps his hand around my

99

throat but doesn't squeeze. "Here's how it's going to go, Pink." His lips are right at my ear, hot breath feathering at my temple. "I'm going to be in charge of punishing. And the fear, we're going to release. Okay?"

I have absolutely no idea what that means, but my body seems to understand. Tingles race all down my skin. My pussy clenches. He presses his lips to my temple and drags them along the skin. Not a kiss. Something hotter. Meaner.

"Wh-what do you mean?" I manage to say.

To my disappointment, he pulls away and frees me, but it's only for a moment. He pulls open his car door and pushes my torso down over the seat. His hand cracks down on my butt, hard.

"Oh!" I cry out in shock.

He squeezes the place he just spanked, rubbing away the sting. My whole body bursts into flames, sizzling under his touch. "You want to be punished? I get to be the guy who gives it. Not you." He spanks the other side, just as hard.

I cry out again, but the pain instantly morphs into heat. Especially with his large palm massaging and rubbing. "Cole," I whimper.

He rubs some more. "Fuck, baby. I love it when you say my name like that."

I don't know what's happening. I mean, I vaguely do, but I'm still a virgin. And this is beyond Advanced Placement sex. This is graduate school level. Is this even sex? I can't be sure, I only know that the thrills running through my body, the lust curling my toes, is enough energy to power a large city.

"Cole." I can't help myself. I don't even say it because he wants me to. I just whimper because I want more. Need more. And I'm not even sure what more means.

"Say *yes, Cole*." He strokes between my legs, but not over my slit. Off to the side, just brushing where I want him to be. He's purposely teasing me. He delivers three hard slaps in a row. "I'm going to do the punishing. Tell me you agree."

My stomach flip flops. Squirms. Excitement rages. "Yeah. Maybe," I agree.

"*Yes,*" he corrects firmly. "You know I need to be the guy who punishes you. And you need me to do it. Right?"

Yes is on the tip of my tongue. He has me mesmerized. All good sense thrown out the window. But I hang on to a scrap of reason. "I'm not sure what I'm agreeing to."

His hand strokes over my ass, kneading and squeezing, circling. He rests his other hand beside me on the seat cushion and leans down to meet my gaze. "I'm going to take care of you, Bailey."

It sounds like a promise. Again, I'm not sure what it means, but I believe him. I believe his sincerity. "Okay," I whisper.

Satisfaction lights his gaze and he pulls up, then slides a hand beneath my knees to pick me up and slide me behind the wheel.

I panic. "No." I try to get out, but he blocks my way. "You're driving," he growls. "Tonight."

My hands flutter to the wheel but I look up at him, pleading for mercy. "I can't."

He catches my face between both hands and kisses me

hard. "You can. And you will." He slams the door and walks around to the passenger side, then climbs in.

"Here." He hands me the keys. "Do you know how to drive a manual?"

"Yes." I drove a Subaru back in Colorado. My mom wanted me to learn on a manual so I'd have that skill. My hands tremble as I put the key in, press the clutch and brake down and start it. "What would you do if I didn't?"

"Teach you," he says immediately. Like it's a no-brainer. He points to the street. "Take a right out of here."

I draw in a shaky breath. His truck is so different from the Subaru or my mom's car, that it doesn't ignite the PTSD as badly. I check that the gear is in first and ease off the clutch. There's a lurch that makes me scream, but then we're on the road driving. I'm breathing hard, my heart beating as I nervously check and recheck the rearview mirrors, but it's fine. There's no traffic.

I'm driving!

Cole directs me up toward the mountains. At first I think we're going to the same secret playground, but instead he guides me to an overlook. "Park it here," he orders and I do, relieved to turn the truck off and collapse back against the seat.

"You did it." Cole's grin is boyish. Happy. It's an incredible look on him, devastating, really. Shifting position to face me, he puts one knee on the long seat cushion and braces the other against the floor. "Now your reward."

In a flash, he grabs my waist and pulls me to my back on the seat, my dress hiked up to my waist.

"Cole!" That seems to be the only word I'm capable of, and in the next moment, I lose the ability to articulate at all, because Cole shoves my panties to the side and presses his mouth to my pussy.

I jerk at the soft contact of his lips against my most sensitive parts. When he uses his tongue, I nearly pop off the seat. He has to pin my pelvis down, hold me in place as he strokes his tongue all up and down my slit, tracing my inner lips, flicking it at the apex, where the clit is supposed to be, but I've never really found it.

Doesn't matter. Cole knows where it is. He tortures me, lapping, sucking, nipping. I squeal and wriggle. Moan and whimper.

My legs thrash beneath him. I'm desperate. It's too intense. I push his head away. "Wait," I cry hoarsely.

I'm reassured by his compliance. He stops immediately and lifts his head, studying my face. "You're scared," he says. Not a question.

My face grows hot. "I don't know. Yes. Maybe."

"But you like it. I can taste your nectar, Pink. Just let go. Take your reward. I promise it will be good." He reaches up and pinches one nipple through my dress fabric and bra, then slaps the side of my breast. He repeats the action with the other side.

My mouth falls open in shock, but my pussy pulses with total glee.

And I don't protest when he dips his head again to return to pleasuring me.

∿

COLE

. . .

I DON'T KNOW how I'm keeping my wolf in check. She's the hottest thing I've ever seen. Face flushed, dark hair fanned out around her head like a storm, eyes wild and glassy. She tastes like all my fantasies rolled into one and I can't fucking wait to watch her go off.

She's fighting it, though.

I lift my head and rub her clit with my thumb. "Do you make yourself come, Pink?"

She shakes her head. "N-not really. But I did... after—"

I raise my brows in question.

"After you kissed me."

Satisfaction explodes through me.

"Oh, babygirl. I fucked my hand so hard that night I almost broke my dick off."

She's shocked, which I love. I guess I have a bit of the sadist in me. I never knew. Or maybe it's just for her. Just for Pink. Because she took all my hate and twisted it around into something sexual. Something painful but beautiful.

Fuck, spanking her was like finding the meaning of life.

I've never felt so powerful. Not in a mean way, either. It was fucking ecstasy. The scent of her arousal filling my nostrils while she made those surprised cries of pain. The fact that she fucking *let* me spank her like that—that she liked it.

And somehow playing that role helps me keep my head. The raging hormones of a teen wolf don't drive me the way they have with other girls. Oh, I definitely want her—to a degree that is painful—but I have the reins on my lust. Bailey turned control over to me, so I can't fuck it up. I have to keep my head.

"How did you make yourself come? What did you do?" I explore her tight entrance, screw my index finger into her channel while I keep tapping and rubbing her clit with my thumb.

She rolls her head from side to side. "I... um... I used my hand."

"Where were you, babygirl? In the shower? On your bed?"

"On my bed," she gasps, arching into my hand. "On my stomach."

I smile at the secret she shared. "Humping your hand?"

"Yeah," she gasps.

I pull my index finger out and work my thumb in, instead. "When I say it's time, Pink, you're going to let go and come. Can you do that for me?"

She nods quickly, like she's eager to comply. "I-I'll try."

"Good girl." I get my thumb fully seated and mold the rest of my hand over her mound, so I can put pressure on her clit. Then I start slowly fucking her with my thickest digit. She's tighter than a fist.

She moans low and soft.

I pump it faster.

Her ass squeezes, belly shudders on a breath. "Cole," she whines.

"Come, Bailey," I snarl, my own need starting to making my vision dome. "You're going to fucking come when I tell you to, and you're going to scream my name."

She comes before I can tell her again. It's glorious. Her

muscles seize and tighten around my thumb in quick pulses as her knees press in on my shoulders.

I barely wait until she's done and then I'm up on my knees, pulling my cock out and fisting it.

For a moment, she's too blissed out to know what I'm doing. Then she freaks out.

"Cole!" she gasps, pushing up to her elbows and staring at the purple head of my dick. I abuse it with my fist, jerking hard. It's only going to take me thirty seconds to blow. "I-I'm not ready for that—"

"Chill, Pink," I snarl. I know what she thinks. That I have my cock out because I want to fuck her with it.

And yeah, I do.

But I'm not going to. I wouldn't push a girl too far. And I'm pissed at her for thinking I'm that much of a dick, even though I know I've given her no reason to believe differently.

"You think I don't know what you're ready for?"

She watches me, eyes still wide.

"I'm fucking my hand, that's all. Pull your dress up higher," I order her. "Show me your tits."

She relaxes, a seductive smile spreading over her face and pulls her mini dress up over her breasts, showing me her sweet little pink bra.

"Take them out." My voice is rough and raw. My cock strains and lurches, desperate for completion.

She shoves the bra cups down and shows me her perfect tits. Dusky-rose nipples top the pretty twin globes.

"Squeeze them." I can barely speak. My eyes are already rolling back in my head with pleasure.

When she obeys, I hurtle over the edge and spurt, christening her belly and tits with my cum.

And then I'm transformed. As soon as the vise of need opens, I freefall into gratitude. Into humility. Even affection. I shove my cock away and rip my shirt off my back with one hand. I use it to mop her clean. Then I put her back together—tucking her tits back in the cups and kissing the top of each one. I trail my lips down her breastbone. Over her belly. I straighten her panties and kiss her mound.

"You okay, baby?"

Her expression goes soft. There's wonder in it, like she had no idea an orgasm could make her feel so good. Or maybe she had no idea what it does to a guy. How much I want to reward her right now for rocking my world.

She nods.

"You sure?" I stroke the outside of her thigh, all the way to her panties. Her skin is so soft and smooth. Touching her is a goddamn privilege. I lower my head again and kiss the inside of her thigh, down by her knee. I kiss a little higher. "You were so fucking beautiful when you came."

It's funny how easy it is to be honest with her in my post-orgasmic euphoria. To drop my armor and let her know the truth—how much I really like her, despite the way this all started.

"Bailey." She hasn't answered me. I think she's probably just incapable still, but I want to be sure. "Talk to me, Pink."

She struggles to push up on her elbows again. "Yeah,

I'm good. I'm good." She looks dazed and disheveled. Beautiful.

I help her sit up, then pull her onto my lap. This is one of those moments when I fucking love driving a classic truck. It's totally sex-worthy. Big, long seat. High cab. Perfect. I joked about it's dual purpose with the guys when I started restoring it.

She sits stiffly on my lap, like she doesn't know what to do with herself. "Come here." I pull her back against my torso until she relaxes and rests her head on mine.

We sit in silence for a moment and reality sets in.

I'm acting like I own Bailey Sanchez, like I marked her with more than my cum. Like I gave her a claiming bite and declared my intentions forever.

But none of that is even remotely true. She's a human. A relationship with her is forbidden. And she's not just any human, but the daughter of my dad's nemesis. He would see this as total betrayal.

"What time is it?" Bailey asks, like her mind has been whirring, too.

I pull my phone out and look at it. "Twelve-thirty. Are you going to be in trouble?"

"Kinda. I don't know. I should get back."

"'Kay." I open my door. I would make her drive more to make sure she's comfortable, but I doubt her ability to be clear-minded and focused at the moment.

Another time.

And there it is: I'm definitely seeing Bailey again.

I have to.

I slide out from under Bailey and leave her in the passenger seat before I shut the door gently and walk around. We drive back in silence. I stop the car at the end of our street and hesitate. I can't pull up with her in the cab again.

"I'll get out here," she volunteers, probably reading my mind.

"Fuck that." I throw the truck into park and hop out. "I'll walk you to your house." I walk around to her side.

She tumbles out and I take her hand. She doesn't move, just stares up at me like she can't believe it. I guess it does seem like I just had a personality transplant.

"Don't worry. I'll be a dick again tomorrow."

The laugh that spills from her lips rings with relief.

"Come here." I cup her face and kiss her lips. It's not the bruising, violent kisses of before, but something different. An apology, maybe. For the dick I've been.

The dick I'll be again.

I kiss her again, then start walking. "Come on. I don't want you to get into trouble."

I walk along, trying to ignore how comfortable it feels to be her escort. The guy who protects her when she's walking down the street at night. The guy who holds her hand.

I stop just before we get to her house. "This isn't over," I tell her, like it's a warning.

And it is.

Her gaze is wary.

"You have sins to atone for. And I'm the guy who's going to make you pay." I point at my chest.

Her lips curl up at the edges like I excited her.

Good.

I excited myself, too.

I can't wait to spank that ass again.

I let her go without any more kisses. "Be good, baby-girl," I say, walking backward toward my truck.

She just stands there, smiling.

First time I've seen her smile like that. So happy and relaxed. Free.

I did that.

Satisfaction rolls through me.

There's not much good in me. Not much I'm good at.

But making Bailey smile just popped to the top of my short term goals.

CHAPTER 9

ailey

THE NEXT DAY, I sit behind the wheel of my mom's Corolla, trying to get up the nerve to turn the key.

It's weird how much I want to do it. Like I'm doing it for him. To please him.

And it also makes my chest warm and gooey thinking about how much he did for me last night. Not the eating me part, although that was mind-blowing. But making me drive. Claiming the job of my punisher.

I'm not sure what I think of that.

You know I need to be the guy who punishes you. And you need me to do it.

It's not hard to see why he might enjoy hurting me. I represent the shit-hole his life is in right now. And he's right, I accept it. Because I want to be punished.

And the fact that it ended with us both satisfied means it's not wrong… right?

I take a gulping breath and turn the key. The car starts and I put it into gear. Back out of the garage.

My mom comes out the front door, her jaw dropped in surprise.

I take my hand off the wheel for a brief wave and drive down the street, all the while taking deep inhalations to settle my churning stomach. I drive through town. Past the stadium. Up to the dirt road where the hidden playground is. I park and get out, ducking through the tunnel of branches to emerge at the secret park. It's even more magnificent in the glow of the morning sun. The striations on the canyon walls serve as nature's giant artwork for a giant open-air living room.

It's beautiful today. This is the time of year people are happy to live in Arizona. Not the suffocating heat of August, when we moved here. We'd be expecting the first snow back in Colorado, but October in Arizona is still warm. I'm celebrating by wearing a pair of short-shorts and a halter top.

I tense when I hear another car pull up.

Maybe it's not as secret as I thought.

But it's Cole who comes strolling through the archway, the lopsided know-it-all grin on his face, his keys flipping around his fingers.

He doesn't say a word, just comes for me and doesn't stop. His body bumps right against mine and he walks me backward, into the roofless building, where he picks me up by the waist and sits me on the smooth wooden table. My purse tumbles to the ground.

"Someone deserves another reward," he purrs.

Oh God.

My pussy clenches. Tummy flips again.

Of course I've been thinking about last night's reward non-stop, but it's quite another thing to repeat it in the light of the day. In an outdoor location where anyone could come up.

Well, maybe not anyone, since it's our secret park. But still. My face grows warm thinking about it.

Cole pries my knees apart and lightly strokes over the seam of my shorts, sending massive flutters through my belly. "Do you want my mouth here again?"

"Um…" My heart pounds. I'm both excited and terrified to do this again in the light of day. "I'm not sure."

Cole cocks his head and raises a brow. "Really?" His voice drips with disbelief. "Well, you know what I'm sure of?"

I shake my head.

"I'm sure I want to spank this ass again." Somehow he deftly flips me over so I'm face down on the table, legs dangling off.

He unbuttons my shorts in the front and gives a swift tug so they fall to the ground. "And I'm definitely sure I want to see my handprints today."

My ass clenches. More flutters explode.

He hooks his thumbs in the waistband of my panties and slowly drags them down. I get the feeling he's taking his time in case I protest, which gives me more confidence.

I believe I can trust Cole, despite everything.

Cool air hits my butt as my panties tangle around my thighs.

He smacks my ass.

"Ow!" It hurts more on my bare butt. My skin prickles and smarts as Cole makes a satisfied growl in his throat. He lightly strokes his palm over the place he just smacked, like he's admiring the curve of my ass.

He smacks the other side. I choke on my breath. "Beautiful," he mutters. He presses one palm into my lower back and delivers five slaps in quick succession.

"Ouch! Cole, stop!"

He does. Or I guess he already had before I said it. He strokes his palm over my ass again and leans his torso over mine to speak in my ear. "Do you want me to stop because it hurts, Pink, or because it turns you on?"

My breath shudders in. I swallow. "Because it's humiliating," I admit. That's really what makes me squirmy and fearful. Not that he'd actually hurt me. Not that he'd take things too far—he's proven he won't. But that I'm surrendering to him, and I'm not sure he's worthy of my vulnerability.

He bites my ear. "We already hold each other's humiliations, Pink. We own each other's secrets."

I pant beneath him, my pussy wet, the bulge of his cock pressing against my bare ass. I close my eyes, the sensations too much. The intensity of his gaze on me way too exposing.

"You already have my humiliation. You saw me get my ass beat in front of the goddamn neighborhood. Your presence next door is a daily humiliation to my dad. To my family."

He doesn't mention that he witnessed mine with Brumgard, too, which I appreciate. That incident has no place creeping into this moment.

"So I'm going to keep spanking this ass as much as I want to, Pink. And I know it turns you on, because you're dripping wet." He shifts his cock away from my ass and slides a couple fingers over my slit.

I gasp.

He's right. I'm soaked. I didn't even know it was possible to be so wet. Had no idea what my body would do to ready me for sex.

Not that I'm having sex with him.

He slaps me again, but it's not as hard, like he's taking mercy on me, or modulating the intensity until he's sure I'm into it. "The way I figure it, you owe me your humiliations, Pink. And I'm going to take all of them, one by one, until you're stripped bare to me."

A shiver runs down my thighs.

I hear the rustle of his pants and I turn around to see him pulling out his cock. "I'm not going to fuck you with it, Pink," he says immediately, like he knows I might freak out again. "You're going to push those sexy thighs tight together and I'm going to run my cock right over your pretty little slit until we both come."

Holy. Crap.

I am so in over my head, and yet it all feels so available. So necessary. My body doesn't require instruction. It already knows this is a total go for me.

"Got it?" he says. He's speaking his normal language of alpha-hole, but I realize he's actually waiting for a green light.

"Yeah," I breathe.

"Good girl."

I don't know why I like it when he says that, except that maybe I am always trying to be the good girl. Thought I was one until the accident.

He rubs his cock down the seam of my ass, then slides it between my thighs, as promised. The velvety steel glides over my entrance and past it, sending shivers of pleasure down my legs. It feels better than his fingers.

He shudders. "Fuck. Way too dangerous," he says.

I'm not entirely sure what he means—maybe that he might actually slide in. Or that he won't be able to hold back. He pulls back and spits on his hand, rubs it over his cock and thrusts between my upper thighs. "You keep these real tight for me, Pink. Can you do that?" His voice sounds deep and gravelly. A little desperate.

"Yes."

He pulls my hips back and cups my mons from the front, exactly the way I hold myself when I masturbate. I moan and rub against him while he fucks my inner thighs in the area I can squeeze them tightest.

"Fuck, Pink," he curses. I like the way his voice breaks, like he's losing control. He slides a finger in me, but I don't think he can concentrate on both of us at the same time. His breath is ragged. After a moment, he pulls back and slaps my ass. He drags my panties off my legs and spanks me again. "Spread your legs, Pink. Wide as you can."

I do it. He grips both my asscheeks and spreads them wide. I never could've expected what happens next. Never knew it was a thing. He runs his tongue from my pussy to my anus.

I scream and try to move but he's holding me in place. "Cole! You can't do that. Ohmygod, please!" I'm embarrassed. Totally insecure and very, very turned on. It feels amazing and so, so wrong.

He lifts his head, but it's only to deliver three hard spanks to one cheek, then he lowers and licks again, circling my anus with his tongue. I whimper, my legs trembling too much to even hold me up.

"I'm going to fuck you here some day," he promises, voice thick. He rubs my back hole with his thumb. "It will be part of your punishment."

"No," I whimper, but I'm about to combust. Excitement trembles everywhere. Flames lick my core.

"Yes, Pink. And you're going to love it. You can't lie to me about that. I taste your juices."

I didn't know that was a thing, either, but I'm sure he's right. My pussy is molten. He holds his thumb over my anus.

"Clamp my dick again with those thighs."

I obey. It seems I will do anything he asks of me. Spread my legs, close them, offer my ass up for a spanking.

I close my thighs as tight as I can again around his cock and he fucks me again, all the while rubbing my anus and making me squirm.

"You're going to tell me when you need punishment," he says. "If you need to let off steam. If you need to cry. Need to feel. And we'll come here and I'll spank this ass red, Pink. And I'll always leave you feeling good. I promise you that." He seems to get tired of the position again. It must be hard for him because he has to bend his knees so much to be at the right level. He turns me around, picks me up and sits my bare ass on the wood of the table.

I squeal, not because the table isn't smooth, but it just feels wrong. He grunts, lifts me back off—the guy is hella strong!—and yanks off his t-shirt. He spreads it on the table, then picks me back up. The moment my ass hits the t-shirt, he pushes me onto my back and slides his hands under my pelvis. When he lifts my hips in the air and licks into me in this position, I cry out and clamp my thighs around his ears, throw my legs over his broad shoulders.

"Cole!"

"Keep saying it, baby." He nips my outer lips, then returns to the eager licking.

"Cole, Cole, Cole," I chant and he laughs against me.

"You gonna wait until I tell you to come this time?"

My brain's getting too fuzzy to dissect his words. Everything is a haze of pleasure and sensation. Heat and desire.

"Cole... Cole."

"Not until I tell you," he warns.

I finally understand. I'm supposed to wait to orgasm. Orgasm on command.

Is that how this works? I've never heard of such a thing, but I'm not exactly well-versed. Turns out there's a lot more than just moving parts.

He shifts one of his hands and works his thumb into my pussy, all the while sucking and flicking with his tongue. "Now, Pink," he says, then suctions his mouth over me, while fucking me with his thumb and finding my back hole with one of his fingers.

I scream.

I shudder.
I come.
Hard.

~

COLE

I'M SERIOUSLY GOING to die. My balls are swollen and aching, my dick is harder than granite. And something about Bailey makes me want to do dirty things with her. I've watched a lot of porn—like every eighteen-year-old male—and right now, I have the nastiest ideas in my head.

When she finishes coming, I shift my arms all the way up to her shoulders to scoop her off the table. I set her down in the center of it and rearrange my t-shirt underneath her. I could give her a verbal command. She's been gloriously obedient, which gives me this heady confidence to do whatever the fuck I want with her. But there's also something hot about not telling. Just moving her body. Like she's a fuck-doll just for me.

And of course, the thrill is always seeing whether she'll let me do it or not. She's into this as much as I am, even though there *is* humiliation. But is it degrading if she wants it, too? That's what she'll have to figure out, I guess. I'm just riding this thing out because I feel like a fucking rock star right now and I haven't even come yet.

I push her to her back, then roll her to her belly. She lets me.

It's fucking glorious.

"Looks like today's the day I'm going to fuck your ass," I tell her.

When she squeezes her butt tight and whirls to look over her shoulder in alarm, I smirk, fisting my erection. "Just the cheeks, though." I straddle her thighs and grip her two asscheeks. She's still tense, so I smack one side. "Relax them, Pink. You can squeeze after I slide my cock in."

She's confused, which doesn't surprise me. I don't think girls watch porn like guys do. Or at least, if they do, it's probably not the shit I've seen.

"Take it easy, babygirl." I pinch a wide section of her ass and shake it. "I'm not going to put it in you. Just between, like I did with your thighs."

She peeks back at me her big doll eyes swimming with heat and vulnerability. "Promise?"

"Promise, baby."

She relaxes and I tuck my cock between her cheeks with a dollop of spit. I push them together around my length, my thumbs meeting over her crack to keep me from popping out as I glide back and forth.

"Fuuuuuuck," I groan. The visual is smoking hot. The sensation, even better. I snap my hips, tunneling through her asscheeks, glorying in this hot-as-fuck act. It feels taboo and filthy. I've had sex with three girls before Bailey, but nothing's come close to this, and I haven't even been inside her yet.

I want to keep it up forever, but it's too late. I was way too horned up when I started to last. "Bailey, Bailey, Bailey, Bailey." I return the favor of chanting her name just before I erupt, coating her lower back with my spunk.

"Holy fuck, that was hot." I don't have anything to wipe her off with, since she's lying on my shirt, so I settle on my side beside her and rub my cum all over her ass. Marking her.

She hasn't moved. I pull her hair back from her neck and bite it. Just a love-bite, although for a moment, my wolf surges to life, like he thinks I'm going to mark her.

As if.

She's a fucking human.

Why does that idea make my body tingle all over?

I settle onto my back and rest my hand on Bailey's ass. She rolls over onto her back and we stare up at the blue sky.

"Next time I want to give you a blowjob."

I choke a little. My cock surges back out of my open jeans. "You can't just say something like that to a guy." I lace my fingers through hers, joining our hands on the table.

"Why not?"

I give a mirthless laugh. "Because now I won't sleep or eat until it happens. I'm gonna be all horned up fantasizing about what those pouty lips of yours look like stretched around my cock."

"Jesus, Cole."

"What?"

"Do all guys talk like you with their gir... partners?"

"Oh." I laugh. "Probably not. Sorry, Straight-As. You get the unedited version."

We fall silent for a moment, then I observe, "It's a good thing you're not in journalism anymore." The truth is, I miss sitting next to her every day. Even though the sight of her used to piss me off, she was always my obsession.

"Why is that?"

"I'd be hard the whole time." It's true, if she were in class, I'd have a tent in my jeans the whole hour.

"Wow. Is it painful?"

"Fuck, yeah, it's painful. And it would be embarrassing as hell." I lift our entwined fingers in the air, staring at this unexpected development. Have I ever held a girl's hand before? I don't think so. I never felt this bond before. This extreme attachment. "You could come back if you wanted. I would make sure he never looked at you, never spoke to you. You should see him, Pink. He gets all sweaty-templed every time I walk into the classroom."

Her hand gets colder.

"Of course you don't want to come back," I answer for her. "Sorry, that was a stupid idea."

"I'm still thinking about doing the newspaper thing," she says. "Rayne and I brainstormed article ideas."

"Yeah?" I realize I don't know enough about this newspaper thing, which is stupid, since even before I kissed her, I made it my business to know everything I could find out about Bailey. "So how will you do it?"

"Well, I don't know. Originally, Bru...Brumgard—"

"—Asswipe," I interrupt when she stumbles over his name.

"—Asswipe was going to assign the class the articles and then I would just edit and put it together. But I figure between Rayne and I, we can write them all."

I contemplate that for a minute. "Nah, you should still make him work for you. Let's email the fucker. Where's your phone?" I demand, climbing off the table and retrieving her purse, which dropped to the ground when I pounced on her. I toss her panties and shorts up, too, because I'm feeling generous. I unsnap the purse and unsheathe her phone, then hand it to her. "Open your email."

"Why?" She's wary, which annoys me. I know I haven't given her reason to trust me, but I want her to anyway. I guess I want it both ways. I want her to trust me while I continue to torment her. I snatch it back from her and swipe my thumb over the buttons to open email. "Pink, when I give you an order, you're supposed to answer *yes, sir*."

She snorts derisively. "In your dreams, buddy."

We turn our heads toward each other on the table and I grin, because it does sound ridiculous. "Yes, *daddy*?"

"Ew." She punches me. "Weirdo."

"Don't pretend you don't fucking like taking orders from me, babygirl. Your body doesn't lie."

She blushes and I take a mental snapshot of how beautiful she looks right now with the pink stain on her skin lighting up her warm brown eyes, picking up the pink swath of her hair.

"Anyway, I'm emailing Asswipe. I'm gonna tell him how it's gonna go."

Her nipples get hard. I swear to fate, they tent her little halter top. (And holy shit—that halter top!) I sprout a chub knowing she's turned on by something I said.

I open her account and start an email to Asswipe, reading it out loud as I go:

Mr. Asswipe,

Bailey grabs my wrist and pulls it down to read the screen where I actually wrote *Brumgard*. She grins and releases it.

As you've noticed, I am no longer attending your class. I'm unwilling to forego my education, however—

I roll my head to grin at Bailey. "Did that sound Straight A's enough?" She smiles back with a warmth I haven't seen in her eyes before. It does something shifty to my chest. "You didn't know I had it in me, did you? Thought I was flunk-out material?"

She smacks my ribs with the back of her hand. "Go on. Let's see what you've got."

Therefore, I plan to continue with publishing the student newspaper. The following are articles I would like you to assign to the class:

I hand the phone to her. "Now you fill them in."

She takes the phone, her eyes still on me, like she's thinking it over.

"He's your bitch, Pink. Treat him like he's fucking staff. You give him the assignments now. Get it?"

Her pulse flutters at her throat, like she's excited by the idea. Or maybe she's just excited by me, because her nips are still hard. I pinch one through her shirt and she jerks and tries to cover it with her forearm.

"Uh uh." I catch both her wrists and straddle her, pinning them beside her head, her phone still clutched in one hand. "These are mine to torture. Remember?"

She shakes her head. "I don't recall agreeing to that."

I shrug. "I'm your punisher. I decide what torment you get."

She flushes and the scent of her arousal drugs me. I

lower my head and lick up the side of her neck, from her collarbone to her jaw. The sound of her soft panting arouses me further.

"If you don't watch out, I'm gonna call in that blowjob right here and now, Pink."

She fake-struggles. "What am I watching out about? I didn't say anything."

Right. She doesn't know I can smell her arousal. She probably can't even scent it, herself, which strikes me as slightly tragic. I make a mental note to watch myself with her. I'm getting way too comfortable.

I drop my gaze to her titties. "Your nipples are hard, little girl. It's turning me on."

"Oh." She flushes some more, lifting her head to look. "I didn't, erm, know you could see that."

I waggle my eyebrows. "Oh, I can. I definitely can." I take pity on her and roll off to the side. "But you have other work to do. Make that list, babygirl."

CHAPTER 10

ailey

SHIT. I think I'm falling for Cole Muchmore. Since last night, hell since our first kiss, I've had a giddy, almost manic bubbly sensation in the pit of my stomach and it won't go away. Is this lust? Love? Infatuation? It wasn't supposed to happen this way. Cole is a jerk—*was* a jerk. I don't know. He's quickly flipping my whole existence on its head.

Which isn't a bad thing.

It's a wonderful, exhilarating, incredible thing.

And that's definitely the problem.

I sneak a sidelong glance at him as I recreate the list of articles Rayne and I came up with from memory. He looks beautiful. His bare, muscled torso is tan and gorgeous in the sunlight. His hair is rumpled and he's wearing that lopsided grin that makes my heart speed up every time he flashes it at me. I could combat his good looks, though. What I can't fight is the way my body feels—both satiated and hungry for more. Every secret place he's been today is still awash with sensations, still tingling with awareness.

What I'm completely exposed to is this protective thing he has with me against Brumgard. I'd like to say I'm a big girl and don't need him to fight my battles, and I think that's mostly true. But it sure satisfies me to have the school bully in my court. To watch him turn his art of intimidation on the teacher who wronged me. I f-ing love it.

So much.

I finish with my list and hand the phone back to him without hitting send. He reads through it and nods. Then types a little more:

We will correspond via email, as I don't want to see you in person. Please have the articles to me in two weeks.

Cole looks at me. "What else do you need?"

"Um, okay. I want to know how we actually print the paper. Like if I need to get quotes on printing and who pays for it. Oh, and how we format it."

"Okay." He returns to the screen. *Also, please let me know how the newspaper will be printed and formatting requirements. I expect to maintain my perfect grade point average throughout this process, and I'd appreciate those letters of recommendation by the end of the week.* Cole arches his brows. "Anything else you want to include?"

He's right. My nipples are totally hard. It turns me on to watch him wield his alpha-hole power. Confidence is sexy. So sexy.

He smirks and tweaks one nipple between his thumb

and forefinger, letting me know he doesn't miss my arousal.

Crap! I am so screwed.

I meant it, though, about wanting to give him a blowjob. I've never done it before, but he's eaten me out twice. And he's been super respectful about not pushing for sex. Or full penetration—whatever. So I want to give back.

And that gives me excited flutters. I like that it's a promise we're doing this again, too. I don't know what our relationship is—especially considering his dad would kill him if he knew about it—but I'm definitely considering us a thing now.

Not that defining relationships ever did anything but box people in.

"Cole?" I don't look at him. I stare up at fluffy white clouds against the pale blue sky.

"Yeah?"

"I wasn't supposed to like you."

"Don't start now," he says, almost immediately. There's no teasing quality to his voice, either. "You would definitely regret it."

Ouch. If my wariness fell away with his promise that we hold each other's secrets, it screams back in full force now. I sit up, wanting to flee as fast as I can. I try to scoot to the edge of the table, but Cole's strong arm bands around my waist and he drags me back to sit on his lap.

"Don't run." It's a soft command, his lips moving against my ear. He bites my neck, then kisses the same place. "I don't want you to run." He shifts the arm around my waist to slide his palm up my side and cup one breast.

"I don't know what we're doing, but I fucking love the way it feels. And so do you. We both need this. Admit it."

Because I'm still butt-hurt, I keep my lips firmly closed, even though he's definitely right.

He releases my boob at my lack of response and turns me on his lap, threading my leg across so I'm straddling him. His strength is stunning. I've never felt so light and petite before. I definitely don't worry about being too heavy for his thighs.

"I'm not going to be your boyfriend, Pink. I won't hold your hand in the hallways or ask you to the prom. You saw"—he gestures in the direction of our homes—"I can't even drive you home without a shitstorm. I'm barely keeping my life together, Bails." He strokes one hand up and down my thigh, as if to soften the harshness of his words. "So don't sign me up for love. Or like or anything. Don't have any expectations of me. All I can promise is what we have. This." He waves his hand at the picnic table and park.

I still want to run. He's being honest with me. I should appreciate it, but instead it's like being broken up with. And I'm way too raw after what we just did for this. I nod and try to swing my leg off, but he catches it.

"Bailey." He catches my gaze and holds it, intensity glittering in his dark eyes.

"What?" I'm pissy, and I don't bother hiding it.

"I wasn't supposed to like you, either. I was pissed. You moved in next door right when things were at their worst with my dad. He'd just been fired and replaced by your mom and he seriously tried to drink himself to death. He'd been prone to drinking and violence since

ALPHA BULLY

my mom left him two years ago, but it got so much worse."

My stomach tightens into a knot listening to Cole. He's baring himself to me—something I never expected.

"Pretty much my life sucked and I wanted someone to blame for it. I picked you. I'm sorry. Nah, fuck that, I'm not sorry, Pink."

I stare, mouth open in surprise, the knot in my stomach moving up and lodging under my ribs.

"I'm not sorry because I *know* we both needed this. I didn't understand my obsession with you then and it came from a dark place, but now—now it seems so clear. The darkness is gone. I satisfy my need to punish you and you release your guilt. We fit. Maybe just for this moment in time, this one blip in our lives, we come together. We find absolution. In each other."

My mouth is dry. I try and fail to swallow. "So... this is just sexual?"

"No way. I've had sex before and it was nothing like what happens with you. Definitely more than sexual." He finds my hands and twines his fingers between mine, holding our hands up by our shoulders, like we're meeting at an invisible wall. "But do we have to define it? I fucking know you feel the same way. Just admit it."

I nod mutely. "I'm driving now. I could always transfer to Cave Hills. Get a boyfriend who's happy to acknowl- edge me in the halls at school."

"But you're not going to."

"No. I'm not going to." For better or worse I'm locked into a twisted dance with Cole. I have to see it through. And it may be messed up, but right now I'd rather see him,

131

have him near every day, in any capacity that I can have him, than go to Cave Hills.

I'm surprised to see relief flicker over his expression. Was he sweating me ending things? That, almost more than his speech, loosens and melts all the places I'd frozen up inside. Is it enough to just have *this*—whatever *this* is?

Maybe. For the moment.

I can't seem to turn away from Cole, even though he's like the car crash you see coming but can't seem to stop. No, bad analogy. Nothing is like that. Even when we crash and burn, Cole Muchmore will have been worth it.

~

COLE

WHEN I GET HOME, my dad's still sleeping on the couch where he passed out last night.

I head straight for the shower. I'm supposed to work at Bo's uncle's auto shop today, but when I saw Bailey take off in her mom's car, I texted that I was going to be late. My phone's blown up with texts from Bo, but I don't give a shit. I wouldn't trade this morning for anything.

I bump into Casey coming out of our shared bathroom upstairs. Her nostrils flare at my scent and then her brows slam down. She grabs a fistful of my t-shirt and pushes me into the bathroom and shuts the door. As if our dad could hear anything in his state.

"What the fuck are you doing?" she whisper shouts. "You have her scent all over you."

I ignore her and peel off my shirt. "Get out, Casey."

"Cole, I'm serious. You can't do this. Are you nuts? Of all the humans you could pick to fuck, you pick her? Do you want to die?"

For some reason, it angers me that she assumes I'm just fucking Bailey. Like she's the usual random human the alpha-holes use to practice sex on. I must show some teeth when I growl because Casey flinches and steps back, the instinctive submission to alpha dominance immediate.

"Fates, Cole," she sounds stunned. Frightened, even. "You really like her."

"Get out, Casey," I snarl.

She skirts around me and opens the door, slipping out. "Cole, you better stop this shit before you get us all kicked out of the pack. We're only hanging by a thread as it is. Alpha Green probably would've done it already based on Dad's fuck-ups if you and I weren't still in school."

Her words hit me in the gut.

"I have it under control." It's a lie, but I'll get it under control. Somehow.

I can't fuck Casey's future up along with mine just because I can't keep my dick in my pants when it comes to Bailey Sanchez. It's not right.

Casey shakes her head as she pulls the door shut and I take her condemnation into the shower with me, washing away Bailey's delectable scent, the traces of my betrayal to my father, family and pack.

Fuck.

CHAPTER 11

 ole

IT'S BEEN MOST of the week and I've managed to stay away from Bailey. I'd like to say I took the space to get my head screwed on straight and now realize there's no way I can keep fucking around with a human, much less this particular one.

But rather than cure me of my obsession, the time apart gets me worked into a frenzy. I think about her all the time. Jack off three times a day to the memory of spanking her ass and fucking those plump cheeks. When I'm home, I watch her window from mine and text her. First I texted to ask if she got a response from Brumgard. Then to tell her that Brumgard assigned the articles. To talk about which article I'd been assigned and tell her I expected her to complete the assignment for me. She sent me a gif of a girl flipping off the camera, which made me laugh. She probably would still write it for me, but I'm actually looking forward to the assignment. It's different knowing I'm doing it for her and her pet project as opposed to Asswipe.

I took the assignment of writing a feature article on one of Wolf Ridge's sports heroes. I'm going to interview Wilde about being team captain and what that entails. It's going to be good.

When I'm at school I'm always looking for her in the hallways. And then when I see her—fuck, when I see her —I always want to throw her over my shoulder and carry her off somewhere to get filthy again.

I settle for winking when we pass each other. Or glaring at her from across the schoolyard. She always feels the heat of my gaze. Always turns and blushes. Rubs a hand over the back of her neck like I made the skin prickle there.

But that doesn't happen to humans—does it?

Today, though. Today she's not in one of her customary dresses. She's wearing those short shorts she had on last Saturday, and it's driving me fucking nuts. I find her after school and cage her in at her locker, making it appear like I'm harassing her. Which I am.

"What the fuck are you wearing?" I growl in her ear.

She turns her face to the side, but not far enough to make eye contact. Just enough to let me see her. "What's it to you?" she sasses.

I press in a little tighter, letting the bulge of my swollen cock contact the back of the shorts. "You don't wear shorts that short at school. Especially not *those* shorts."

She frowns. "What's wrong with these shorts?"

"Don't play dumb, Bailey. Last time you were in those shorts, I took them off you. You fucking know what you're doing to me. I'm going to smack your ass twice this shade." I tug the streak of pale pink hair framing her face.

Her laugh is low and husky. A little nervous. The scent of her arousal drifts up between us, making my nostrils flare.

She glances past me, though, where my friends are standing by the lockers eyeing us. "You'd better go."

"Don't want to." I mean, I *really* don't want to. My need for her seems to be getting stronger and stronger. It must be because we're approaching the full moon. It's nuts because she's not even a she-wolf. I shouldn't have such a hard-on to get with her. It's like my wolf wants to mate already. "Fuck," I mutter out loud. This means I'd better stay away from her over the weekend. I might lose control, which would have devastating consequences. It's bad enough I might need Austin to fucking babysit me to make sure I don't go seek her out.

"Meet me after practice," I blurt, even though any of my friends could overhear with their shifter hearing. Even though meeting her anywhere public is a bad idea and we sure as hell can't meet near our houses, either.

Her eyes dilate like she's excited. "Where?"

I think fast. "Here. At the school. Six p.m. I'll wait for you by the locker rooms. You can get in through the door on that side of the building."

Pink is driving regularly and has a car now—a used VW bug that sent my dad into a fury about the "spoiled human bitch" when he saw it.

"Okay." She ducks her head to hide a smile. She's been

137

super cool about not letting on we're an item, which I'm grateful for.

"Spank you later," I murmur and wink, resisting the overwhelming urge to smack her ass before I walk away.

Practice is a total fucking blur. I don't even know which drills we worked on or if I did what I was supposed to. My head was stuffed with Bailey the whole time.

After practice, I send Casey home with Austin and take a long, thorough shower. When six o'clock rolls around, everyone's cleared out. I had this idea of pulling her into the locker room and ravishing her over a bench, but it occurs to me that every fucking member of the team will smell human in here tomorrow if I do.

Football field is no better because anyone could see us.

I step outside to wait for Bailey by the back door, still trying to figure out where to take her. She shows up with a big In-N-Out Burger bag, which she holds out to me. "I thought you might be hungry."

The scent of food hits me hard. I'm fucking starved. Casey and I have been living on ramen noodles and frozen burritos since our dad lost his job—shit I can buy with the money I earn working at Winslow's auto shop. Even so, if any other person tried to offer me food, I might have beaten them to a pulp.

But from Bailey? I don't know, from her it means something different.

And the thoughtfulness of it knocks me on my ass.

I grab the bag and look inside at the two burgers and two fries and two shakes. Cute. She doesn't know how much a shifter eats. "These are all for me, right?" I flash her a grin. The stars in her eyes when she looks at me make me feel like some kind of hero.

The guy I've never been.

And that's when I realize: the In-N-Out Burger food will cover all scents. That shit can make the cab of my truck stink for a week. If I bring it into the locker room, no one's gonna smell human. Just meat and fries.

I take Bailey's hand and tug her inside. My stomach's growling, but I drop the bag of food on the bench. "This deserves a reward." I cup her ass and squeeze.

Her breath quickens, eyes dilate. I glide my lips over hers. Not the mean, demanding kisses I've given before, but something more sultry. More exploratory. I let my palms roam, over her ass, up her sides underneath the shirt. She's trembling already. There's something in her scent, though. I try to distinguish it from the food.

Then I figure it out. "You're nervous."

Of course she's nervous. She's a total noob and I laid a lot of expectation on this encounter—blow job, spanking —every fantasy I've jacked off to all week.

Vulnerability flickers over her face.

"Am I going too fast?"

She stops breathing altogether, still looking up at me with doe eyes. Trapped in the headlights doe-eyes.

I release her and pick up her hand. "We don't have to do this. Come on, let's go for a ride, instead." The last thing I'll do is pressure a virgin. That's not me. I want a girl willing and enjoying herself.

Scratch that. I want *Bailey* willing and enjoying herself.

I have zero interest in other girls at the moment. And I don't want to unpack what that means.

Without waiting for her to agree or disagree, I make the decision I know is right and grab the food and lead her out. I'll save locker fantasy for another day.

~

A MIXTURE of relief and disappointment runs through me as we walk hand-in-hand to the parking lot. There are a few other cars in the lot—who knows, maybe they belong to the janitors.

Cole was right; I was nervous. Stupid me had to lay the expectation of a blowjob and now he's expecting it and I panicked because I don't know what the hell I'm doing. You lick it like a popsicle was the advice Catrina had shared a million years ago but somehow that advice seems a bit lacking now. Surely there's more to it. And why didn't I just GTS—Google That Shit—before today?

So now I feel a little bit foolish, mostly relieved, and a million times melty inside at how sweet Cole was about it.

Where's the alpha-hole posturing? I thought he'd order me on my knees and tell me what to do.

Okay, actually, that's hot.

And it might make all this easier than me pretending I know what I'm doing.

Cole releases my hand to fish through the take-out bag and pull out his burger as we walk. "This was really fucking thoughtful, Pink," he says with his mouth full. I take the bag so he can use both hands and reach in for a single fry.

Cole shakes his head "You're like a fucking kitten, all dainty with your food. Humans are so delicate."

"Humans?"

"I mean girls." He's still wolfing down the burger, which is almost gone. "It's cute, Pink." He pops the last third of the burger in his mouth. "You're adorable."

I try to hide the glow of pleasure his words bring. "Holy shit. Did you even chew?"

He grins. "I don't remember."

I pull his fries out and juggle the bag to put ketchup on them before I hand them over.

"You ketchuped my fries." He sounds surprised.

"Oh. Sorry—do you not like ketchup?"

"I *do* like ketchup. I like you working to please me even more."

I stop walking in exaggerated offense.

Cole shoots that lopsided smirk my way and holds out his hand to take mine. "Don't get pissed, Pink. I promise all the rewards."

I take his hand. We were heading toward his truck, but he stops and looks around the parking lot for my car.

"Let me drive your new baby?"

I fish my keys out of my purse. "Sure. Seeing as how you let me drive yours. *Forced* me, actually."

"And rewarded you," he reminds me with a waggle of his brows that brings heat to my cheeks.

And what a reward it was.

My body heats at the memory.

"Have you named it yet?" Cole asks as he swings into my compact car and adjusts the seat back as far as it goes.

I snort. "Do you even fit?"

"I've been asked that before," he boasts and I roll my eyes.

"I haven't thought of a name I love yet. What do you think?"

He turns the key, considering. "You could call it New Start. You know, for driving again and moving here."

Grief rolls over me like a wave. The moments are shorter now. Quicker. I could lean into them and go back to the depressed state I lived in for the last six months or I can just let them pass through me and acknowledge that it's part of the process. I let it pass and swallow. "*New Start* it is. Good name."

Cole pulls out of the school parking lot, appearing pleased. I never would've pegged him for a name your car kind of guy, but he does seem to love his truck.

"What's your truck's name?"

"The Captain," he says proudly.

"First name *The,* last name *Captain*?"

"That's right, smart ass."

"It's a great truck. You rebuilt it yourself, right?"

"Yep. Bought it for one hundred bucks off Bo's brother Winslow. Their uncle owns Wolf Ridge Body Shop—the one down on the corner of Mountain and McGee?"

I nod even though I don't really have my bearings in Wolf Ridge yet. I only just started driving this week.

"I work there on weekends with Bo. Have since we were twelve. When there's no paid work to do, I work on

The Captain. It's almost ready for a new paint job, but I haven't had the money."

I wince, even though he's not being a dick at the moment. Not accusing me and my mom of being the source of his lack.

Cole gets on the highway. "Where are we going?"

"I know this great gelato place in Cave Hills. Our mom used to take us as a reward for our patience after clothes shopping. You gonna eat the rest of that burger?"

"Nope." I hand over the last third of my burger. "I should've bought you two."

"I can eat four of those and not even blink, babygirl. Where do you think I get my stamina?" He winks and I roll my eyes, trying to will away the blush I sense crawling up from under my t-shirt collar.

Every encounter with Cole has been so far out of my playbook I can't even categorize them. But this one? This feels like a date. He's taking me for gelato. And while it's not nearly as exciting as getting spanked and blowing him in a locker room, it does crazy things to my mind. Or is that my heart?

Crap.

I am so screwed.

We go in and order fancy gelato. I get dark chocolate orange and he gets mint chocolate chip. I know better than to offer to pay, even though I also know Cole's hurting for money. He pays and we take it outside to sit on the patio overlooking the busy street below.

"It feels good to be out of Wolf Ridge," I say. Even though it was only a twenty minute drive, Cave Hills feels more like an ordinary suburban city while Wolf Ridge manages to have the insular, small-town feeling.

It's ritzy. It's the northern part of Scottsdale, so there's money here and I brace myself for a moment, fearing Cole will misconstrue my comfort here.

But he agrees. "Wolf Ridge gets so old. The same families have lived there for more than a hundred years. Everyone's always in your business. I can't fucking stand it."

It occurs to me that he's probably been the object of the town's scorn since his dad's plummet from grace. Which isn't his fault. No wonder he's been so bitter and rebellious.

"Are you planning to leave? You could get a football scholarship somewhere, right?"

A shutter slams down over his expression. "Nah. I gotta stick around for my sister. But no one leaves Wolf Ridge, really." He shrugs like it's just this accepted reality.

"But do you *want* to stay? I understand about Casey… with your, um, dad situation. But what about when she graduates?"

"Shut up, Pink." There's no smirk. Cole's back to alpha-hole and he clearly resents my questions.

But this is what he does, isn't it? He pushes people away to avoid the shame of his situation. Or the despair of how stuck he feels.

He picks up our empty ice cream cups and throws them in the trash. "We'd better get back," he says flatly. "I don't like to leave Casey home alone too long."

By *home alone*, I assume he means home with his dad.

144

I get up and follow him to the car. Cole starts the engine, not looking at me.

"Cole, I think you and Casey should get some help. It's not right that you're not only fending for yourselves, but afraid to be at home. If the authorities got involved, you and Casey would be taken away from your dad. I know he's having a hard time, but he's a shitty father right now."

"Shut up! Shut up, Pink." He slams his fist down on my dashboard and the plastic cracks. "*Fuck!*"

I sit in stunned silence and stare at the crack.

"I'm sorry," he croaks.

"No, I'm sorry," I whisper. "I don't mean to upset you. I just—"

"He didn't used to be a bad father," Cole chokes out, his voice breaking. "He didn't used to be."

Tears flood my eyes, spill down my cheeks. Cole's pain slices me to ribbons. Of course he still loves his dad. Things aren't black and white. Good and bad. His good dad is still there somewhere, under the alcoholism and violence.

Cole finally looks over at me, eyeing my tears. "There you go with those tears again," he says bitterly. "Why do you do that?"

"What?"

"Cry for me."

I dash at the tears with the back of my hand. "I can't help it."

He reaches for me, wraps his fingers around the back of my head and pulls my face right up to his. He doesn't kiss me though. Just studies my face with a mixture of rage and wonder.

145

I tense, wondering which one will win out.

And then he pounces. Attacks my lips with his, same as the first time I cried for him, but this time we're stuck in the tiny cabin of my Beetle. His tongue fucks my mouth, fingers twist in my hair. Everything about it is rough and brutal.

Passionate.

He tries to pull me toward him, but I'm caught by my seatbelt. Instead, he settles for crushing one hand over my left breast while he continues to kiss the hell out of me.

And then, just as suddenly, he releases me.

I fall back in my seat, breathless.

He stares at me with eyes that look golden in the streetlight instead of their usual brown. "You're lucky we're not in The Captain or I'd fuck you so hard you wouldn't walk straight tomorrow."

And as if that's the definitive answer to our discussion, he turns forward and starts the car, backing out of the parking place.

I'm a tangled mess in the passenger seat. Heat pulses between my legs and flushes through all my veins. Tears still smear my cheeks and my lips are bruised and swollen from his onslaught.

As he pulls back on the highway, he says, "I didn't mean it that way, Bailey." He doesn't look at me, just keeps his eyes on the road. A muscle in his jaw flexes. "I don't force myself on women. I want you to know that."

I straighten myself out, adjust my clothing, sit forward in my seat. Why am I still breathless? "I know," I puff out. "You've proven that, Cole."

"It does something to me when you cry." His voice is

146

strangled and I detect confusion in his voice, like he's surprised by his own reactions. "I mean I always want to fuck you, but then you go and cry for me and I want to fucking *consume* you." He shakes his head. "Nevermind. That doesn't make sense. Am I scaring you?"

"No," I whisper. It's only partly a lie. He's exciting me.

As we drive back, Cole offers, "My mom ran away with the Wolf Ridge High math teacher."

"Oh shit." I cover my mouth with my hand.

"Yeah. Talk about a fucking scandal. They left town together and we haven't heard from her since."

"Not even you and Casey? She hasn't tried to contact you?"

"Nope." His face is a brutal reflection of bitterness and hurt.

"That's fucked up."

"No shit." Cole pulls into the school parking lot. "So that's when our household collapsed. My dad started drinking. It affected his job. You know what happened next."

"He got fired and they hired my mom in." I whisper. "And Jesus, what are the chances of us moving in next door? I keep thinking with how small Wolf Ridge is, the realtor should've warned us or something. I mean, didn't she know? Seems like everyone knows everything here."

Cole grimaces. "Oh she knew. She probably figured it was my dad's due punishment. When the Wolf Ridge Brewery shut down for three weeks, three quarters of the town went on reduced pay. He was and probably still is the least favorite pa—I mean, town—member."

"Well, that's fucked up. Someone should get him some help instead of judging and condemning."

"He wouldn't take anyone's help. My dad's a stubborn asshole when it comes to admitting any weakness."

"Hmm." I don't say how much that sounds just like him, but he picks up my tone.

"Shut up, Pink." He doesn't sound pissed, though. He turns my car off, leaving the keys in the ignition.

∼

COLE

I TOUCH the crack I put in Bailey's dash. "I didn't mean to hurt New Start. I will fix it for you, I promise."

The approaching full moon is definitely getting to me. I swear I nearly marked Bailey back there. One minute I locked lips with her, the next my wolf was right at the surface. Like my canine teeth elongated to giving her a mating mark.

I've never had that happen before. Not even at the worst of the raging puberty hormones.

I have to wonder if it's because there's more at play here than sex. I don't just want to fuck her—Bailey's under my skin. I want to hold her hand and make her laugh and hear her dreams. And yeah, fuck her until she screams.

And fuck if any of that is possible.

She's human.

Not a suitable mate. Definitely forbidden. And the daughter of the enemy.

That doesn't stop me from wanting her.

But not during the full moon. I need to keep away until it's over. Just a few more days.

"Thanks," she murmurs. I eye her, trying to gauge how mad she is over it. I can get Bo's uncle, Greg, to order a new dash right away, but I don't have the money to pay for it. I might be able to talk Greg into spotting me, but that's a big *might*.

"Are you coming to the game Saturday?"

"Of course," she says, like it's always been her and me. Like she didn't flip me off last time I asked her to come. Well, *told* her to come. Her easy acceptance makes me warm and itchy. Like I need to be careful because someone's going to get hurt.

Both of us are if I don't put the brakes on this.

Trouble is, I don't want to.

"You'd better," I say. "I'll be looking for you. But I can't hang out after the game. We're doing team building all weekend," I lie, putting up barricades now while I still have a little control.

Disappointment flickers over her face before she hides it. She rubs her tattoo. There's a trace of grief in her scent that I don't quite understand.

"Next week, though, I'm getting you alone," I promise. "I'm going to punish you for wearing these shorts. You don't put them on again except on dates with me. Got it?"

She rolls her eyes and gives my arm a shove. "I don't take orders from you." It's a show. She's excited. My whole body's attuned to hers now. The disappointment is gone, replaced by the light reverberation of giddiness.

Good.

She wants it as badly as I do.

Now all I have to do is make it through the full moon.

The rest of this shit I can figure out later.

I step out of her car and catch sight of someone else in the parking lot, walking to a familiar red Honda Civic.

Adriana.

And she definitely sees me getting out of Bailey's car.

Fuck.

Double fuck.

Hopefully she keeps her mouth shut.

Somehow, though, I know she won't.

BAILEY

I STAY after school to talk to the counselor about my college essays. When I walk out to my car, I find a plastic grocery bag of papers tucked under the windshield wiper of New Start.

I take the plastic bag out and open it. Inside is the stack of newspaper articles. I look around, even though it's highly unlikely the person who left these is still here. Was it Brumgard? Or Cole?

I pull my phone out of my backpack and check my texts. My heartbeat speeds up when I see there's a new message from Cole.

Of course it was him.

Left the newspaper articles on your car.

I look toward the football field. I've purposely been

parking in front of it—like an idiot—to catch glimpses of
him. The team spills out onto the field, taking a few laps
around it as warm up. I spot Cole right away. I'm good at
picking him out now. The broad shoulders, lean build.

It always feels like he's staring right at me when I see
him from a distance. Even now, I would swear he's
clocking me as he runs. I stand there watching for a
moment until he runs by the fence close to me. He doesn't
take the turn, just plows straight into the fence, bending it
from the force.

"Jesus, Cole. What the hell are you doing, man?" his
buddy Wilde says before he looks up and sees me. "Oh."
It's a low, disapproving syllable. He leaves without another
comment.

"You're lucky there's a fence between you and me
right now," Cole says, fingers twining in the metal loops.
This is his form of flirting in public—throwing out subtle
threats that others will take as bullying, but I register as
sexual aggression.

"Am I?" The hardest thing for me is not responding.
Acting bored, or even feigning discomfort, when really I
want to let him pounce on me instead of that fence. Paw
me with those large hands. Lick and bite me like a half-
feral beast.

I'm disappointed he's going to be busy this coming
weekend. Saturday is Catrina's birthday. If I ever truly
needed punishment, it would be then.

He points a finger at me now as he slowly retreats and
starts jogging backwards. "Better watch yourself, Pink."

"Oh I'm ready," I call back and his face splits into that
lopsided grin I find so damn attractive.

Warm and giddy, I climb in my car, which I hate myself for loving.

I guess it wasn't just fear keeping me from driving before. I made some silent vow to Catrina and not driving was the hardship I had to endure to make sure I never hurt someone again. To make sure I remember every day why I don't drive.

But Cole's in charge of my penance now. He made me drive. It's on him. At least there's no ice here, no snow or slippery roads to cause another accident.

At home I go through the articles. It doesn't look like Brumgard bothered to read or grade them. Some of them are useable. Some are absolute garbage. I pick up Cole's and read.

It's good.

Really good.

It's an interview with his friend Wilde about what it's like to be captain of the football team. I expect a bunch of cliché or cocky shit, but instead Cole captures some vulnerability and earnestness. Wilde apparently works on team building on and off the field. He suffers from imposter syndrome; he doesn't use that term, but that's essentially the gist of it. He talks about all the shoes he has to fill from past generations, including his own father, who was also a football star at the school. It's a thoughtful, interesting feature article and I have to believe Cole did a good job on it for me.

I pick up my phone and text him. *I'm impressed. Best article in the stack. Thank you.*

He texts me back, *I can be Straight A's too.*

If only you applied yourself.

I can apply myself. I can apply my hand to your ass.

I roll my eyes and smile. Then, because Cole is there, because he has my back, I open an email to Brumgard.

Thank you for the articles. I selected several for publication. Please have the following students email me their stories so I don't need to retype them. I have the quotes on printing. Can you get a purchase order from the school to cover the costs?

Making a teacher my bitch. I'm living a whole new world under the tutelage of Cole Muchmore and his cocky alpha-hole ways.

Maybe getting molested by a teacher has a silver lining. I'm learning to assert myself in all kinds of new ways.

And I definitely have Cole to thank for it.

CHAPTER 12

 ailey

COLE TOLD me we couldn't get together this weekend.

That doesn't stop me from checking my phone or watching the street outside for his truck after the football game.

I went to watch, as promised, and this time I actually enjoyed myself. Rayne and I still sat in the back, but I felt more comfortable. Even though the entire rest of the school still snubs both of us, the star of the team wanted me there.

I saw him looking for me. I swear I knew when he spotted me, too. And he played gloriously.

Lakeside had no chance against Wolf Ridge High. Our school absolutely trounced them. I'm starting to see why people enjoy sports around here so much. There's never the disappointment of losing.

But now the game is over. My mom is still working on her laptop at the kitchen table, and I'm home, thinking about Catrina.

About what we'd be doing if she were still alive, how we would celebrate her eighteenth birthday. I lie on my bed and do what I vowed not to do—torture myself by opening up my old Instagram account. And there she is, her beautiful smile lighting up picture after picture of the two of us together and with friends. An entire photo-documentary of our years from seventh grade when I opened my account until she died.

I cry until I run out of tears and then I finally get a grip.

This isn't doing me any good, and if I keep squatting in this hole I've dug, I'll never get myself out of it. I roll off the bed and slip on a pair of flip flops.

I need to get out of the house, and I know exactly where I want to go.

"I'm going for a drive, Mom," I call as I head to the door.

"Bailey? Wait, where are you going?" My mom leans in her chair to see me through the doorway to the living room and catches sight of my puffy red eyes. "Baby, what's wrong?"

I choke back a fresh sob. "Nothing. It's Catrina's birthday. I'm going for a drive."

Concern etches her forehead. "Okay, angel," she says like she thinks it's a weird idea but isn't going to argue. "Be safe."

I wince. "I'll try," I mutter and shut the door.

The sun has already set and a huge full moon is rising

over Wolf Ridge. It's the Hunter's Moon, Rayne said yesterday. Whatever that means.

I get in my car and drive up to the abandoned playground. Cole said he liked to come here when he needs to get away, so it seemed like a good place. Although coming after dark is a little creepy.

The light of the full moon casts everything into an eerie glow. But it's so bright I don't have to take out my phone to see where I'm going.

I sit on a swing and give myself a push, gradually building height until I'm soaring, the wind rushing across my skin, the sense of falling and swooping soothing my heartache. I close my eyes and melt into it.

And that's when I hear the growling.

My eyes fly open and I nearly piss my pants. Three giant wolves stand in a semi circle in front of me, teeth bared, fur ruffed. The unearthly growls send terror zipping up my spine.

I try to scream, but no sound comes out. I think my diaphragm's stuck up in my throat.

I grip the rusty metal chains tighter, pumping my legs harder, like that will somehow get me out of here. Like if I swing high enough, the seat will just detach and fly me back home.

Shit, shit shit. I had no idea there were wolves in these parts. I mean, yes, it's called Wolf Ridge, but I honestly didn't know there was a real danger. Isn't the Mexican gray wolf originally from this area on the extinction list?

The wolves show no sign of leaving. They've decided I'm dinner and they're waiting for me to get off the damn swing. My whole body starts shaking like a leaf. Silent tears fall down my cheeks.

What can I do? My phone is with my purse at the base of the swing. I can't stay here and swing all night.

Yes, yes I can. That's what I'm going to do.

Twenty minutes later my thighs burn so badly they're cramping and my palms are so sweaty I can barely hold on to the chains. And my plan isn't working. The wolves below me are restless. First they sat down to wait, but now they circle, coming in closer. One lunges and nips at my legs when I swing through the lowest point. I scream, trying to hold my feet as high in the air as possible.

On the swing back, it snaps its powerful jaws around my foot. My scream echoes off the canyon rocks. Pain slices through where a tooth punctures the top of my foot and I'm yanked forcefully from the swing. I land on my back on the ground and the wind gets knocked out of me, abruptly ending my high-pitched scream.

Panic roars through me. I need to run, escape, but I can barely stagger to my feet and I'm surrounded by three snarling wolves.

And then out of nowhere, a fourth wolf appears, launching into the ring and tussling with one of the first three.

I scream again, trying to back up, but I can't. The wolves have me boxed in. The newer wolf, an enormous tan and white beast, springs free of the tussle and positions itself in front of me, like it's claiming me as its food. Like it wants to fight the others for the right to eat me.

Oh God. I have never been so screwed in my life.

And I've also never been so certain I don't want to die.

After the accident and my grief over Catrina, I often wondered what was the point of going on. Now, I'm quite positive I have so much to live for. Exploring this thing with Cole is at the top of my list.

And now I may not have the chance. No, fuck that. I'm getting out of this.

The wolves continue to snarl and snap at me and at the new wolf. Four more wolves slink into my line of sight. Christ, how many of them are there in this pack?

I look around for a weapon within reach. There isn't much, but I see a large rock. I slowly stoop to pick it up with shaking hands, but one of the wolves launches at me and knocks me to my back. I scream again.

The latest arrivals jump in and there's more fighting. Maybe this is two packs fighting for their meal? Fur flies, snarls fills the air.

The tan and white wolf literally stands over me in a show of dominance and territory claimed. Eventually, the first three wolves drop the fight and trot away, turning every once in a while to snarl at the winning pack.

I'm still afraid to move. The wolf standing over me isn't facing me, he's facing out, but he still could turn and sink those terrifying teeth into my throat at any second.

All the growling stops. Apparently the winning wolves don't need to show me dominance. They're already sure of their dinner. I blink in the moonlight. Is one of the wolves wearing a chain with dog tags attached? Like military dog tags?

And then suddenly there's a blur and a snapping of bones and Cole's crouched over me buck naked. He scoops me up into his arms and lifts me easily. Looking down at one of the wolves, he says curtly, "I'm taking her to your cabin."

Like talking to wolves is a normal thing.

Holy fuck. Cole just changed from a wolf!

Am I high?

Am I hallucinating?

It takes me more than a minute to believe what I just saw with my own eyes. My brain's trying to produce a more plausible explanation, but there isn't one. Cole is a wolf. *They all are wolves. Werewolves.* And the moon is full.

Holy shit, does this mean I'm still dinner? But a different kind of supernatural dinner?

As if he senses my fresh surge of fear, Cole looks into my eyes for the first time. His glow amber instead of their usual brown. "Hey, hey, hey. You're safe now. Don't be scared, babygirl. I've got you."

He strides with long steps toward my car, stopping to pick up my purse from the ground on the way. His feet are bare, like the rest of him, but he doesn't seem to notice the rocks and rough ground as he walks. He just takes me around to the passenger side, sets me on my feet and wrestles my sweatshirt off me to tie around his waist and cover his junk. Holy shit—his very erect, very long—I snap my eyes back up to his face.

"You're bleeding." He scans me. "Where?"

"I don't know. My foot, probably. I got bit." I think I'm going into shock, if I'm not there already. None of this is making sense.

Cole shakes my keys out of my purse and pops the locks. He opens my door and lifts me into the seat.

After he climbs into the driver's side, I warble, "A-am I going to turn into a werewolf now?"

He lets out a puff of surprised laughter, but immediately sobers. "No, baby. We're a different species. It's not a disease. Not contagious." He takes off out of the parking lot, screeching down the dirt road.

"Tell me you don't eat my species."

Now he does laugh. "Only in the way you love, Pink."

I pull my knees up to my chest, my ruined Chucks resting on the seat as I hug my legs.

"Hey." He lays a hand on my knee. "Are you okay? Do you need a hospital or can we take care of your injuries at Austin's cabin?"

Austin.

The other wolf. Holy shit! Those other wolves are kids from school!

Ice sluices through my veins. My brain tries to chug forward to assimilate all this and then falls off a cliff and crashes.

"Bailey?"

"Huh? Oh, um, no. I don't need a hospital. Unless I need a rabies shot or... sorry." I realize that probably sounds super offensive.

"S-so you're a werewolf, huh?"

"Wolf shifter, yeah."

"Wolf shifter. Is that the same thing as werewolf?"

"Werewolf is not the preferred term. It's what humans call us."

"Right, totally." I hug my knees tighter.

"Bailey? You hanging in there? You're not scared of me are you?"

Am I scared of him? No. Definitely not. I'm experiencing a huge sense of betrayal at not knowing this whole town are actual fucking wolves. But Cole Muchmore just saved me from a pack of them, so I'm not scared of him, in particular.

Still, I say, "Should I be, Cole?"

He glances up through the windshield at the full moon and utters a low curse.

"Cole?"

"You're going to be okay, baby. As far as those assholes know, you never saw anyone shift, right?" He glances away from the road to send me a warning look. I notice his hands strangle my steering wheel.

"I never saw anyone shift," I repeat. "Which assholes?"

Cole makes a distinctly wolfy sound in his throat. A growl that makes the hairs on the back of my neck stand up. "That was Bo's brother Winslow and his buddies. They're dicks. They had no right to terrorize you like that." His knuckles go white on the steering wheel and a muscle in his jaw flexes. "I would've fucking killed that asshole Ben for biting you if I weren't outnumbered."

He's been winding around back roads for a while, but now he pulls down a long dirt driveway that dead ends at a small cabin.

"And then your friends came to help?" I'm still trying to figure this all out. My brain is still partially stunned from the fright and shock. "Austin and who else?"

"You know, the alpha-holes: Bo, Wilde, Slade. It's the full moon, the whole pack goes for a run. Listen, you're not supposed to know any of this, Pink. If our alpha finds out you know, I'll be in deep shit and so will you." He parks and gets out.

A shiver runs up my spine.

I don't even want to ask what *deep shit* means in this context.

And yeah. My boyfriend is a wolf-shifter. This night couldn't get weirder.

~

COLE

BAILEY CLIMBS out of the car and winces when she puts weight on her injured foot. I scoop her up in my arms and carry her to the door. The key is hidden where it always is, sitting on top of one of the porch rafters. I unlock the door and let Pink hobble in while I find a pair of jeans and a t-shirt in the front hallway bins.

Shifters always keep extra clothes available. Every shifter car has clothing in the trunk. Cabins like these are meant as a stopping place when the wolves are out on a run, and are fully stocked with clothing, food and supplies.

And it's a good thing Austin's dad is the town physi-cian, because I know there will be a decent med kit here. I find it in the bathroom and bring it out. Pink is sitting on the sofa, with her shoe and sock off. Her foot is already swollen and bruised and she has one deep puncture wound.

Seeing it nearly makes me shift with fury.

I like Winslow okay. I owe him for helping me with The Captain and giving me a job, but he and his friends

RENEE ROSE

can be real cocksuckers when they're together. When they
were in high school and we were still small, they used to
beat the shit out of us just for fun.

I don't know if Winslow thought he was doing me a
favor by picking on Bailey. I'm sure Bo wouldn't have told
him that our relationship is more complicated than bully
and victim. Maybe he was just pissed to find a human in
our stomping grounds. That was my bad for bringing her
there, although I can't possibly regret it because of what
we shared there.

I give her some ibuprofen with a glass of water, then
pour rubbing alcohol in the puncture wound, which makes
her shriek louder than when Ben bit her.

"Sorry! I'm sorry, baby." Fuck. I had no idea it would
hurt her so badly. I can't risk her getting infected, though.
Human wounds can get ugly if not treated. We learned that
in health class.

After I mop it up, I lick the wound with my tongue.
Shifter saliva has healing properties, especially for wolf
bites; it's part of our mating bite biology. I'm hoping she
heals fast.

"What the fuck were you doing out there after dark?
Are you fucking nuts?" I snarl, even though I'm pissed at
myself, not her. I go to the kitchen to find an ice pack in
the freezer.

"How was I supposed to know there would be a pack
of insane wolves breezing through?" she demands back.

I prop her ankle up on an ottoman and arrange the ice
pack over the top of her foot.

Maybe it's the moon, but she looks so fucking beautiful to me right now. Her hair is a mess, face stained with

tears, but those bright eyes and pouty lips make me want to kiss the hell out of her. I stalk over and bury my fingers in her hair in the back, then wrap my fingers and pull.

"What happened last time you were out alone in the dark?"

She sucks in a breath, her eyes darting to my bulging erection and back to my face. "The big, bad wolf got me." Her voice is soft and husky, eyes dilated black.

"He did, didn't he?" I purr. All the rage from finding her under attack, hearing her screams while I was running through the woods and fearing for her life, it all channels into sexual energy now.

I want to do all the things to her.

Every. Last. Dirty. One.

"What do you think he's going to do this time?" I pick her up and flip her to her knees on the couch, her torso folding over the backrest, her foot still resting on the ice on the ottoman. She's wearing a pair of jean cutoff shorts that her ass fills out to perfect completion, but I reach around the front and unbutton them.

I smack one cheek first, then tug her shorts and panties down. My handprint is already blooming on her cheek and I bend over and kiss it. The scent of her arousal hits me hard and goes straight to my head. My wolf snarls at the surface like he wants to mark her.

I give my head a shake and back away. "Seriously, though. What made you think that was a good idea? Even if you didn't know about wolves, is going to a dark, deserted place at night a good plan, Pink? You're a smart girl, genius level, even. What were you thinking?"

"It's Catrina's birthday." It's little more than a whisper.

I go still. Shove my wolf way down. "Fuck."

"Don't stop, Cole." She's pleading. Begging for my help with her guilt.

I slowly wind my fingers in her hair again and tug her head back. "Push your ass out for your spanking, Pink." I make my voice sound harsh. Unforgiving. The way I used to talk to her. I slap her ass once, then position myself better to hold her head back and spank at the same time. Then I deliver a real spanking. Hard slaps alternating right and left. After about ten, she starts squirming and whimpering. I would stop in a heartbeat if she asked, but she doesn't, so I go on, spanking away until her ass is good and pink. Then I go nuts on the reward. I lift her hips to slide her panties and shorts off over her knees, then push her legs wide. With a thumb in each juncture of where thigh meets ass, I spread her, licking into her delicious nectar.

She shrieks and trembles, but I push her pelvis up against the back of the couch and pin it there so I can lick the fuck out of her. I lick from clit to anus and back again. I made my tongue hard and pointy and penetrate her with it. I suck and bite her labia.

It's too much for me, though. My teeth descend. I throw myself backward to get away from her before I do something irreversible and trip over the ottoman on my way. The sound of me spilling to my ass jerks Bailey's head around.

"Cole!" I can tell by the way her eyes widen in fear that I'm not me. My eyes are probably yellow. Teeth are down.

I look out the window at the moon.

Bailey's too smart for her own good. "What happens at the full moon?" she asks, her voice raspy, probably from all the screaming.

And the lust.

I shake my head, getting up. I need to keep my distance from her.

"Do you lose control? Are you dangerous?"

I give a pained laugh. "You could say that."

"What happens?" She's still in position, like she wants me to come back and lick her some more. Finish her off. Of course she does. She must be in at least half as much agony as I am.

I shove my fingers through my hair. "There's a lot of… sexual tension."

Her eyes round, but not with fear. With interest. She gets off the couch and comes over to where I'm standing near the window. "Maybe I can help with that."

She drops to her knees in front of me and I groan.

"Bailey." I know I shouldn't let her do this. I should lock her alone in one of the bedrooms until morning, but it's too late. I'm already unbuttoning the jeans and freeing my staggering erection.

And I want to be gentle. I swear I do, but the message doesn't get through to my body. I grip the back of her hair and hold her head in place as I feed my cock into her waiting mouth. She makes a surprised sound as it goes in, but then she swirls her tongue around the underside and sucks on the way out.

"Bailey. Fuck. Fates. This is insane." I try to tell myself to let go of her hair. Let her drive, but I can't. If anything, the more excited I get, the tighter I hold her, the

167

faster I pump into her mouth, barely stopping myself from ramming the back of her throat.

"You give such good head," I praise her. I'm in ecstasy and pain right now. Dying to come, but never wanting it to end. I don't know if there's something magical about her mouth or just that she's Bailey and she's willing to give this to me, but I've never felt anything so good in my life.

"Oh fates. Oh fuck. Oh fates." I go too deep and gag her a couple times, then somehow force myself to pull out.

"Are you all right?" I pump my cock with my fist, examining her face for clues that she's enjoying this.

Her eyes are watering, but she nods.

"Can I keep fucking your mouth, beautiful? It's so fucking good. Best thing I've ever felt in my whole life."

She reaches for my cock herself and guides it in her mouth. I try to let her lead, but it only lasts a second, and then I capture both sides of her head and fuck her relentlessly. I know it's not comfortable for her. I'm big and I'm being way too rough and controlling. But she's a fucking superstar because the next thing she does is reach for my balls. The minute she starts squeezing and massaging, I go ballistic.

"Bailey, fuck!" I shout. By some miracle, I manage to pull out before I come, spilling down my pumping hand and onto the floor. I drop my head back and close my eyes, still fisting my cock. "Oh fates. That was insane. That was so good, Pink." After several heaving breaths, my eyes pop open. "You never came, did you, babygirl?"

To my utter shock, she drops her fingers between her legs and touches her bare pussy.

I growl. Despite the fact that I just came, my cock

lengthens again.

"Cole, will you…"

I wait, but she doesn't finish. "Will I what, Pink? Lick your pussy? Spank your ass some more?" I drop to my knees facing her and bring my fingers over hers, then shove hers aside to work her wet pleats myself. "Will I spank your pussy?" I give it a little slap and she shrieks.

"I want to go all the way," she says in a small voice.

"Fuuuuuck." I fall back on my heels, afraid to touch her while I contemplate that thought. Then I blurt the very next thought in my head. "There are condoms here."

She's blushing.

"Austin's dad's a doctor. He gave us all the sex talk when we were like twelve and basically told us we could use this cabin to sow our wild oats and that it would be stocked with condoms. I swear that's not why I brought you here, though."

She laughs, but then the smile slips away from her face. "Have you brought someone here before?"

"Never," I say immediately, then flash her a smirk and tackle her to her back. I pin her wrists beside her lovely face. "I like your jealousy, Pink," I murmur right before I claim her mouth.

Five minutes later, we're dry humping on the floor and she pushes me away. "Can we spend the night here?"

Excitement rises. I've never wanted to spend the night with a girl before. The sex I had was kids fooling around. It wasn't the kind where you want to hold a girl afterward. But yeah, Pink's different.

"Yeah, I'm sure we can."

"I need to text my mom that I'm spending the night

with Rayne," Bailey says. Then she turns back with wide eyes. *"Rayne's a wolf?"*

"Ish." I say, wincing a little at explaining this not-so-nice part of our culture. "She's defective. Bad genes. You can tell because she's so small. She hasn't ever shifted."

Pink's lower lip juts out in a sad face. "That's why kids are mean to her? That's awful!"

"I know. It sucks. But she might eventually shift. She's young, still."

Bailey picks up her phone and texts her mom. I borrow it to text Casey, telling her I'm not coming home and she should go spend the night with one of her friends. She was probably planning on it, anyway. She tries to be gone as much as possible.

"Done," I say, handing the phone back to Bailey. "First one to find the condoms wins a prize!" I jump to my feet and go charging off to search the bedrooms. I hear Bailey's musical laugh following me.

"Found them!" she shouts a few minutes later from the bathroom.

I crowd in behind her. "What's that?" I snatch the bottle of lube from her hands and look at the label. "Damn. Dr. Oakley really set up a little sex den for us here, didn't he?"

Bailey smacks my arm and laughs, blushing. I pull off her t-shirt, then my own. Turn on the shower. Bailey watches me shuck my jeans, then unhooks her bra and drops it to the floor.

"You okay?" I settle my palms on her waist and slide my hands up. "Still hurting?"

She shakes her head. "I feel good," she whispers.

"Good." I pick her up to straddle my waist and carry her under the spray of water with my lips locked on hers.

It's a good thing I already came or I wouldn't be able to handle the sensation of her slippery skin rubbing against mine. The sight of her naked tits shifting in front of my face.

I pin her to the shower wall and feast on one of her nipples, sucking, nipping, tugging until she wriggles against me. Then I move onto the other one. While I do, I get filthy with my hands, tracing into her ass crack and making her jump and squeal when I find her anus.

"Oh my god," she says breathlessly. "What's your fascination with my butthole?"

"Everything." I bite her neck, push a little on her tight sphincter to get it to partially open.

She sucks in her breath and squeezes it tight.

"I'm an ass man, and you have a perfect ass. Plus I like how squirmy you get when I touch you there. And"—I drag my mouth up the column of her neck and suck her earlobe—"I'm your punisher. And assholes are where naughty girls have to take it."

Bailey lets out a full-on sex moan. The kind you hear women make in porn clips. The kind that makes me go *rock hard.*

"I *am* going to fuck this ass, Bailey," I warn her, since she's obviously into the punish-y vibe. "Maybe tonight, maybe later. But you're going to take it in the ass from me."

She squirms, rubbing her hot little clit against the root of my cock.

Fuck, I can't wait any longer.

171

I turn off the water and get out, still holding my girl. I pretty much never want to put her down. Like, if we're vertical, she should be straddling me at all times. But right now, we're getting horizontal.

I grab a towel and wrap it around the back of her. "You grab the condoms and lube," I tell her and she giggles as she leans over to grab them, rubbing her wet breasts past my face again.

I carry her to a bedroom and drop her on her back. For a moment, I just stand on my knees and stare down at her. She's like a divine gift from the moon goddess, this lush, healthy human virgin offering herself up to me.

"Are you still wet?" I ask, slowly rubbing my thumb over her slit. I already know she's still wet; her scent engulfs me, intoxicates me. "Plenty wet," I say. "But I don't want it to hurt." I open the bottle of lube and spread a generous amount around her entrance and her anus. I put on a condom and lube it, too.

Then I shake my head at Bailey with mock authority. "So I'm thinking… good girls get their cherries popped missionary style." I flip her to her belly and smack her ass. "Bad girls take it from behind."

I work my thumb between her cheeks and tease her asshole until she starts pumping her hips on the bed. "Spread your legs, Bailey," I order hoarsely. My words come out thick with need. I kneel behind her and rub the head of my cock over her entrance. She's tight.

Super tight.

I pause and screw a finger into her instead, stretching her open to add a second, then a third. "You gonna be a good girl and take my big dick, Pink?"

172

"Try it again," she encourages.

I apply pressure to her entrance again and this time the head slips in. She gasps and tightens, and I stop moving to give her time to get used to it.

"You okay?"

She gives a tiny nod. "Yeah."

I brush her hair back from her face to see the side that's visible. Her eyes are closed, mouth is open. I stay still until she relaxes and starts pushing her hips back to take me deeper.

"That's it, babygirl." I don't dare let myself indulge in celebrating how good her tight pussy feels squeezing my cock like a fist. Now I'm cursing my bright idea of turning her face down, because I can't watch her expression. I keep my focus on her, watching for signs of discomfort.

"Cole."

"Yeah, Pink?"

"Let's do this thing."

I laugh and shove the rest of the way in. She gasps but finishes on a moan. I tangle my fingers in the back of her hair and make a fist. "Like that, baby?"

"More."

Fuck, yeah.

I ease out and then push back in, checking my force at the last second to keep from slamming deep. Now I can't stop the ripple of pleasure from running through me.

I'm awash in sensation: her scent up in my nose, the visual of her face down on the bed, the tight squeezing of her cunt around my dick. And all this under a full moon. It's like being on ecstasy. I've never felt so good. So powerful. So... happy.

Fates. I'm happy.

I could be in deep shit with the pack and my dad for what I'm doing right now, and I don't give a fuck. Nothing's ever felt so right in my life.

My control starts to slip. I curse and release her hair, dropping my hands beside her head to brace myself and get a little more leverage. I snap my hips, slapping her ass with my loins, pushing in to the hilt with each thrust.

She grunts, her body sliding up until her shoulders hit my wrists. And now I have her pinned in place. Every thrust goes deeper, her cries grow louder. My vision blurs.

I fuck her fast and hard, making the bed slam against the wall, the mattress bounce with our weight.

Bailey's making those porn sounds and my balls are drawn up so tight I can feel them in my low belly. My thighs shake. My teeth descend but I vow not to bite her.

Even though her bare shoulder practically begs me to.

"Bailey," I croak.

"Oh my gawd, Cole."

"You'd better fucking come when I do. Are you ready to come?"

"I don't know," she whimpers, reminding me she's a virgin. She's never finished with a cock inside her before.

That's enough for me to get my bearings, close my mouth around the teeth and focus on her pleasure. I pull out and she whimpers.

I grab her hips and lift them until her knees come beneath her to support her. When she tries to stand on her hands, I push her torso back down. "Ass up, Pink." I slap one buttcheek and stand on my knees behind her. I push into her juicy entrance again and grip her hips so I can fuck hard.

I get deeper this time and it's glorious. I can't slow down to enjoy it though. The moment I'm in, it's over for me. My fingers dig into her flesh and I pound into her, forgetting to be gentle. Forgetting she's a virgin.

Worst of all, forgetting she's human. If I hurt her, it will last.

She soaks my cock, though. And when I yell, *now*, she comes all over it, her muscles pulsing around my length as I shoot my load into the condom.

My teeth leak the serum wolves use to permanently mark their mates, but I keep my mouth closed, my canines away from her flesh.

We both pant, our bodies still locked together, a sheen of perspiration coating our skin. Fuck, I think I was way too rough with her. I pull out and dispose of the condom, then find a washcloth, wet it and bring it back.

Bailey's collapsed onto her belly on the towel on the bed, her naked body a glorious sight. I wipe between her legs and up her ass crack, cleaning off the lube and juices.

"Talk to me, Pink." I roll her over.

She blinks up at me, contentedness radiating from her. "I'm good. So good. Are you?"

Relief pours through me. "So good," I agree, falling down beside her.

And it's true. For the first time since my mom left, probably since long before that, I'm soaring. Happy. Fulfilled.

Like I just found my calling and it's making Bailey Sanchez scream.

CHAPTER 13

ailey

I WAKE up every time I stir in the night because I become instantly aware of the large, muscled boy-man lying beside me. I mean wolf-man.

It's a pleasant awareness. Every time I roll over, he shifts, too. Following me. Tossing a thick arm over my waist and pulling me back against him.

I'm spooning with Cole Muchmore.

If anyone told me this moment would happen a month ago, I would've laughed in their face.

When morning comes, I wake to find Cole propped on his forearm, staring down at me.

"Oh! Um, hi." I cover my mouth with my hand to hide my morning breath.

"Hi."

"How long have you been, ah, studying me?"

"I don't know. A while." His brows are furrowed.

"Are you worried about me knowing? You know, about the wolf thing?"

He draws in a slow breath. "Not about *you*. But yeah, kind of. Trying to figure out what I'm going to say if Winslow and his friends tell the alpha about what happened last night." He rubs his jaw. "I don't think they will. They shouldn't have fucked with you like they did. They'd be punished for that. It's forbidden to alert the human world to our existence and cornering and attacking a girl at a playground is kind of a violation of that law." He traces one of my eyebrows with his thumb and I melt.

"Who's the alpha?" I ask.

Cole's lips purse together and he doesn't speak for a moment. "I trust you, Bailey, but I think I should shut up about all the inner workings of the pack."

I try to hide the hurt those words bring. I almost would prefer alpha-hole Cole saying, *Shut up, Pink.* Sincere Cole, honest Cole, flays me alive. Because even though we're getting closer emotionally, he's still holding us apart. He thinks he has to.

And maybe he does.

"How's your foot today?" He snatches the blankets off me, then growls, his eyes flashing yellow as they sweep over my bare body. "You're naked."

"So are you." My face heats but I rake his body over with my eyes, too. He's like one of those marble statues of the Greek Gods. Solid muscle. Beautiful.

Then he sees my foot and the moment's over because it's swollen up and purple. "Fuck, Bailey! Is this what happens with humans? It gets worse before it gets better?"

"What happens with shifters?" I ask, but I'm already remembering how quickly he healed from the beating his dad gave him. Now it makes sense.

"Almost everything heals overnight." He gingerly picks up my foot and licks the puncture wound. I sure am glad for his sake we showered.

"Does that help?"

He shrugs. "I hope so. Our saliva has some healing properties." He gets out of bed and goes to the bathroom. When he returns, he has a glass of water and more ibuprofen. I pop the pills and swallow.

Cole crawls over me. "What about the rest of you, Pink? Sore?" He brushes his thumb between my legs.

A shiver runs through me. "A little tender."

"Let's see how your ass fared." He rolls me over. "Nothing!" he exclaims gleefully. "Your ass has shifter healing abilities."

I giggle until he slaps me and I swallow the sound with my gasp.

"I still owe you a punishment, Pink, for wearing those goddamn shorts to school." He slaps me again, this time catching more of the back of my thigh and I squeal.

"Ouch! That hurt, dammit."

He slaps my cheek. "Funny how that works." He drops to his butt on the bed, leaning against the headboard. "Lie over my lap like a naughty human, and I'll show you what happens when you make a wolf jealous."

"Why would you be jealous?" I protest, but his dominance sends thrills of excitement through me and I climb up to get in position, even as I argue with him. His cock juts out between his thighs, stiff and angry-looking.

After last night, I'm emboldened about my ability to give head. I mean, basically I was just a receptacle for his dick, right? Not much to it. I kneel beside his lap and grab the base to give the head a lick.

"Oh fates," Cole curses. "What are you doing?" His voice sounds strangled.

"I would think it was obvious." I lower my mouth over his length, taking him into the pocket of my cheek and stroking my tongue around the side.

He pinches one of my nipples and tugs. "Are you trying to make it up to me?" His breath is coming quick and hard now, his cock strains in my fist. He smacks my ass, then grips the cheek hard. "Trying to get out of your punishment?"

"Never," I purr and slide my mouth over his cock again, taking him a little deeper.

"Good girl," he growls and pushes my head down too fast. I choke and back up quickly. "Sorry," he mutters, but pushes me again, this time gripping my hair to pull me back at the last second before I choke. It's unbelievably hot to me. I moan around his dick, which seems to get him even more excited. He starts pushing and pulling my head faster. "Take it, Pink. Take my big angry cock. Because this erection is all for you, baby. You've made me hard since the day you moved in wearing those cutoff jean shorts you had on last night. And that really pissed me off."

He grips my hair even tighter, pushes and pulls my head with brutal force. I hear the frustration in his voice, the anger. The desperation.

"I wanted to put you on your knees and stuff your

mouth with my cock every fucking night. I wanted to stuff your ass with my cock."

His words shock me as much as they turn me on. If I hadn't seen the other side of Cole yet, I'd be afraid right now, but I'm sure of him. He doesn't push even though he talks a mean game.

"I smell your arousal, baby. You can't hide shit from a wolf. Every time you get turned on, I know it. Right now, you're dripping for me."

I moan around his cock again and he growls, his jerks becoming erratic. He pulls me off just before he comes, pumping his cock with his own hand as he spurts all over himself.

"Fuck, Bailey. That mouth is insane." He grabs the top sheet and quickly mops up the mess. "Now I want that ass right here." He points to his lap with his cockiest grin.

I'm flushed with heat and beyond excited, but I guess I'm feeling ornery, too. "Make me," I taunt.

He chuckles. "Easy." And it is easy for him. One tug and I'm over his lap. He pins both my wrists behind my back and spanks me ten times fast.

I whimper because it was a little more than what I bargained for.

Cole puts his fingers between my legs and strokes slowly over my soaking folds. "You like to feel my strength, Pink? Or do you even realize how much stronger shifters are than humans?"

It hadn't fully sunk in until that moment, but I suddenly remember every time he's lifted me and carried me with zero effort.

And yeah. It does turn me on.

"That's why sports are so big at Wolf Ridge!" I exclaim, just realizing it, and he laughs.

"That's why, baby. We have to hold back and pretend to lose half the time."

I want to ruminate more about that, but Cole starts spanking me again, another set of ten that sets my ass on fire. "You're serious about this spanking," I gasp when he finishes.

He chuckles and kneads my ass. "Definitely. This ass was made for spanking, Bails. And I was made to spank it."

He slides two fingers into me. I'm definitely still a little sore, but it also feels wonderful. I hike my hips up to take him deeper. Of course he has to go for my asshole then too. He pushes the little button, making me clench and squeeze. He removes his fingers and starts spanking me again. My ass is hot now. Tingling. Definitely smarting, but the pain only amps up my desire. He continues with this game, finger-fucking me, then spanking for two more rounds, until I'm wriggling and moaning over his lap. I want him to finish me now. Make me come.

"Cole," I plead. "I want you inside me."

He slaps me extra hard. "Oh yeah?" His voice has that thick, raspy quality that tells me he's losing control, too.

"Only place you're going to take my cock is in that ass. Are you ready for that, pretty girl?"

Um…

How would I know? Yesterday I didn't know how to give a blowjob or what it's like having my cherry popped. Maybe I should get all my firsts over at once. Give them all to Cole Muchmore. Hasn't he proven himself worthy of them?

"Okay." My voice quakes.

"Yeah?" Cole sound surprised, but he springs instantly into action. He lifts me off him and arranges me in the center of the bed with two pillows under my hips. And that's when he begins the worship of my ass. Squeezing it, rubbing, pulling my cheeks apart and licking my anus. He fingers me while he licks my ass. He spanks me. He spanks my pussy!

I'm breathing hard, rolling my hips from side to side, humping the pillows. Cole dribbles lube between my cheeks and rubs it around my asshole. He pushes until one of his fingers, maybe his thumb, breaches the tight ring and enters me. I moan. It's intense.

And embarrassing!

I reach between my legs and find my clit.

"That's it, Pink. You pleasure your pussy, and I'll take your ass."

I moan my agreement. Gradually I get used to the sensation of having his digit inside me, filling and stretching me. Just when I'm starting to really enjoy it, though, he removes it.

I heard the slick of more lube rubbing over flesh, probably his cock, and he pushes at my entrance.

I whine and squeeze my eyes closed.

"Bailey, take it. Stop resisting, baby."

I don't know what he means, but I take a deep breath and force myself to relax on the exhale. It works, because he starts to stretch me wide.

"Ow..." I protest. The stretch burns a little.

Cole drops more lube to the place we're connected and eases forward more. The moment his head is in, I feel relief. The rest of his cock is easier, although the intensity of being so full, so filled, overwhelms me.

"Are you using those fingers, Bails?"

I like his new nickname for me. I start working my fingers again between my legs. My pussy is swollen and gushing wet. My own fingers slip in without me even meaning to fuck myself with them. I press the heel of my hand over my clit and dip them in over and over again.

Cole holds my hips and buttfucks me. There's something enormously humiliating about it. And the equal parts discomfort and pleasure make it seem to go perfectly with spanking—a punishment. Cole's owning me with every stroke. Showing me he's boss. He's in control and there's nothing I can do about it.

I don't mean truthfully; I know without a shadow of a doubt he'd stop if I asked.

But that's the game we're playing.

The game we both love.

He puts a little more force into it, bumping my hot buttcheeks with his loins when he goes in. He stays in and gives short, quick pumps, bumping me every time.

I want to come. I'm past ready, but it's harder with my ass stretched wide. I usually tighten everything up when I orgasm, but I don't dare with his cock buried inside me.

Cole's breath grows ragged. His fingers dig into my hips. "The naughty little human is getting her ass fucked hard, now, isn't she?" His rough voice comes from a million miles away. I'm already halfway in orbit.

"Whose cock are you taking like a good girl, Pink? Who owns this ass?"

"Cole's! You do." I'm babbling too. We're both drowning in the dirty talk and the incredible intensity of the act. My ass definitely belongs to him and I feel thoroughly punished. Naughty and also redeemed. Cherished and desired.

He pulls out and comes all over my ass. I shove my fingers in my pussy and come all over them.

And then Cole's lips are all over my back, across my shoulders, at my neck. I love this part as much as the rest of it. Without it, I might question my own sanity for letting a guy degrade me. But this is when he's grateful and giving. He makes sure I'm okay. Takes care of me.

I know this even before he rolls me over and peers into my eyes with that watchful intensity. "You good?"

I nod, happily. "Really good."

A slow smile spreads across his face. "Me too."

COLE

I FEEL like I just had a personality transplant. I'm cheerful and happy. Optimistic about the possibilities the future might hold for once. We get up and I work on erasing the evidence of our presence in the cabin—changing the sheets on the bed, and throwing this set in the washing machine. I can come back and put them in the dryer later. Or stay. I guess Bailey can and should drive herself home. Alone.

I don't want to be separated from her, though.

I walk her out to her car, my fingers laced loosely through hers. "I don't want to let you go home. I want to tie you to that bed and keep you here forever." Bailey's gaze shines with wonder. I stroke the backs of my fingers across her cheek.

I want to give her something that means something to match what she just gave to me, but I have nothing, so I settle for my kiss.

It's a good one. Open mouthed but slow. Full of promise and praise. I don't want to stop kissing her, but I know she needs to get home.

I open her door and watch her slide in behind the wheel. "I'm climbing in your window tonight," I blurt as I shut the door.

She laughs and rolls down the window.

"I'm serious. You'd better leave it open for me." I point a stern finger. "I'm gonna be needing to get inside you again on an urgent basis. Like every fucking night. Understand?"

When she looks doubtful, I lean in on the window frame. "It's happening. I'm gonna climb in your window and hold my hand over your mouth while I fuck you from behind. Your mama will never know I was there."

She blushes. "Jesus, Cole!"

I love when I shock her.

"Leave it open," I warn again and walk toward the cabin.

I turn around at the door to watch her start the engine and leave. Only after her car is completely out of sight do I go back in and finish tidying up.

Then I strip out of Austin's clothes, fold them neatly back up and lock the cabin. My truck is still back on the mesa, and now I have to run in wolf form in the daylight.

I'll catch hell if anyone sees me, but it was more than worth it.

My addiction to Bailey just got a hundred times worse.

CHAPTER 14

 *ailey*

"So am I literally the only human in Wolf Ridge?" I ask Rayne Thursday evening while sitting outside Dairy Queen. I picked her up after my visit to Planned Parenthood to get on birth control.

"Shh." She lowers her head and voice even though there's no one else around. "Shifters have acute hearing. Always assume someone's listening."

I duck my head, too.

I tried to keep it a secret from Rayne that I knew. Cole said I shouldn't tell her, or she could be in trouble with their alpha, too, and he said that burden should be his alone. But I have too many questions and my time alone with Cole... well, it hasn't been spent talking.

He wasn't kidding about sneaking in my window. Two out of the last four nights he's visited me after midnight.

Just like he promised, he figures out all kinds of ways to hook up without making noise.

And yes, they usually involve his hand over my mouth, which is hot for more than one reason. I like when he restrains me, when he manhandles me. Especially now that I know what he is. That he's fifty times as strong as I am and really could do anything he wanted to me. I also love the taboo of screwing in my bedroom with my mom just down the hall. I've always been a good girl, so being bad with Cole is the most thrilling thing I've done.

"No. It's like twenty percent human."

"And none of the other humans know?"

Rayne shakes her head. "It's forbidden. The old pack law says any human who finds out has to be killed. Obviously that hasn't been enforced in over a hundred years. At least, not that I've heard."

"Okay, so how long has this pack been here?"

"Since before Arizona became a state, but after it was a territory. Back when this was all the Wild West. The original pack settlers were cowboys and ranchers."

"Like gun-slinging cowboys?"

"Nah. We don't need guns. Plus we maintain a low profile."

"So what happens to a human now, if they find out. Like what would happen to me?"

Rayne's face clouds with worry. "I don't know. Sometimes a leech is brought in to wipe a human's memories of us."

I cock my head. "A leech?"

"A vampire."

A violent shudder runs through my body. "Vampires are real, too?"

Rayne nods.

"What else?"

She blinks at me. "Other shifters. Different species."

"Like what?"

"You name it. Fox, bear, lion, panther. Even some rare ones like owl. And supposedly there used to be dragon shifters, but I guess you only believe that if you believe in dragons."

"Mind. Blown."

"Okay, I spilled. Your turn. Are you and Cole..." She raises her eyebrows up and down as a finish to the sentence.

I nod, blushing. "Yeah. I got birth control today." I show her the packet of pills they gave me to start.

"Was it good?"

I blush some more. "So good. I had no idea how good it could be."

"Jealous. I mean, not of Cole. Just of having sex." Rayne blushes, too. "Well, one thing they probably didn't tell you at the doctor's office is that shifters don't carry STDs. So you don't have to use a condom once you're on the pill."

"Well, that's a relief, I guess." Although the thought of Cole having sex with girls in the past makes my gut burn with jealousy. I open my mouth to ask who his past girl-friends have been, but think better of it.

It's hard enough to navigate this new thing between Cole and me. I don't need to bring his past lovers into the mix, too.

CHAPTER 15

 ole

PACK MEETINGS FALL on the Sunday before the new moon.

Since I turned eighteen in September, they are required for me, which sucks, because I'd much rather be figuring out how to get alone with Bailey again.

My dad's presence is also required, even though he's a lemming these days. He managed to stay semi-sober today and the two of us drive over together in my truck.

As soon as I get there, though, shit blows up.

Alpha Green and Sam Drake, Adriana's dad, are huddled together near the front, and both turn to look at us when we walk in. "There they are," I hear Mr. Drake say. His face and neck are red with anger.

He marches over to us and Alpha Green follows. Mr. Drake points a finger at my chest. "I'm going to rip your dick off, Cole."

My dad snarls, his eyes changing. He lunges for Drake.

"Enough!" Alpha Green puts so much alpha command into the word that the entire congress goes still in submission. He lowers his voice. "We'll take this to a private room." When Mr. Drake starts to protest, he says, "For the sake of your daughter."

What the fuck?

My brain is combusting. I was worried about being called out for being with Bailey. What the fuck does Adriana have to do with anything?

The moment we get alone in one of the meeting rooms, Mr. Drake punches me in the jaw. I go down, lights dancing before my eyes. I hear two snarls: one from my dad, and one from the alpha.

I bounce back to my feet, but keep my fists and eyes down to show my surrender.

Alpha Green has Mr. Drake pinned to the wall by his throat. "You *will* get your temper in check," he snarls.

"What is this about?" I ask.

"Yeah, what is this about?" my dad repeats.

"As if you don't know," Mr. Drake snarls.

"I don't." I keep my tone flat and mild.

"Adriana's pregnant," he hurls at me.

I blink, still calm. "And?" I'm bordering on being a smart ass here, but seriously, does he think it's mine?

"And she said you knocked her up."

"Is that true, son?" my dad scowls at me.

Now I lose my cool. "She said *I*... No. Fuck no. Definitely not."

"Watch your language, boy," Alpha Green snaps.

"Are you denying you had sex with my daughter?"

My neck heats. This is so not the conversation I ever wanted to have with any girl's dad. "Well, no. But it was one time! Last year!"

Drake lunges at me again, but Alpha Green throws him back against the wall. "That's bullshit," he shouts. "She's been out with you a dozen times this month. She told me you were dating."

I gape.

"Cole?" My dad's voice is hard. "You have been out a lot of evenings this month. If you're lying—"

"I'm not lying," I say, with exasperation.

"Who were you out with?" Alpha Green asks.

"Give me your phone," my dad insists, holding out his palm.

Fuck. Why didn't I delete my texts with Bailey?

I have her listed in there as "Pink" but my dad will totally know who it is. Not only will I be in deep shit with our alpha for having a relationship with a human, my dad will be utterly destroyed. Like lose his shit destroyed.

"Who were you with?" Alpha Green puts alpha command in his voice and my resistance evaporates.

"Bailey Sanchez," I mutter, unable to resist the alpha pull.

Fuck!

"Denise Sanchez' daughter?" Alpha Green asks with surprise.

Shame over betraying my dad nearly drowns me, especially with the condemning way the alpha's looking at me.

"What?" My dad snarls, his eyes lighting up with yellow. "You're dating that spoiled little brat next door?"

Fuck.

Fuck. Fuck. Fuck.

"Relationships with humans are forbidden, for one thing," Alpha Green says, even though his own son recently married a human.

For another, I'm a shitty son. He doesn't say that part, but I hear it implied.

"You're dating a human and Adriana?" Mr. Drake demands.

"No! Not Adriana. I told you. Not since last year." The man's an idiot.

"My daughter's not a liar."

Agree to disagree.

"I told you to stay away from that girl." I can't decide what's worse. My dad drunk and furious or semi-sober with this malevolent gleam in his eye. Like he's going to do something bad, really bad, to Bailey and her mom. Or to me, but I don't give a shit about that. I just can't have this turning on Bailey. I can't let our alpha ask if she knows about us. He'd smell a lie and the results for Bailey if he knew could be disastrous.

"How long have you been dating the human?" Alpha Green asks.

I need to make them all forget about Bailey.

I hold my hands up to Mr. Drake. "Due respect, your daughter lied. That pup is not mine." To Alpha Green, I say, "I'm not *dating* Bailey." I turn to my dad and offer the only explanation I can give to diffuse this situation. The one that hasn't been true since the first time I touched Bailey. "We're not dating; I'm evening the scales. Using her." I affect my most ruthless shrug. "I took her V-card and used her up. And she took it, because I'm alpha and she's human. She didn't stand a chance." I can't look at the disapproving faces of Alpha Green and Adriana's dad. I just direct the lies at my dad, whose purple face starts to relax. The yellow leaves his eyes. "When I'm done playing with the human, I'll leave her on her knees. Her mom ruined you. I'm ruining her."

A slow smile spreads over my dad's face. "That's my boy." He thumps a heavy hand on my shoulder.

I'm nauseated. I want to puke. But this is the way I save Bailey.

"Is that the way you treated my Adriana?" Mr. Drake tries to lunge at me again.

"For fuck's sake!" I throw my hands in the air and appeal to our alpha. "Are we done here? Not my pup. I'll take a blood test to prove it."

Alpha Green appears disgusted by all of us. "We're done. Get in the hall for the meeting." He pushes out of the room and I follow, tight on his heels. I have my blinders on, trying to block out any more shit coming from my dad or Mr. Drake so I don't register the small figure leaning over the drinking fountain at first.

One of the kids playing outside while the adults meet has come in for a drink.

No.

She lifts her head and shoots me a death glare and my stomach lurches into my ribs.

Rayne.

Fucking Rayne the Runt just heard every lie I spewed about Bailey.

~

BAILEY

"HE'LL LEAVE me on my knees," I repeat back hollowly. I glance at the screen of my phone, where a new message pops up.

Bailey, don't listen to Rayne. Let me explain.

It's the third one from Cole. The first two were just that he had to talk to me. Now they make sense.

Rayne sits on my bed, crying the tears that I can't quite find.

I'm too shocked. Too emptied. Too shattered.

She wipes her eyes. "I'm sorry. I hate being the messenger, but you have to know."

I nod mutely.

"And the thing about Adriana?" I don't know why I even care at this point if he fucked her, but I need to know.

Rayne shrugs. "I don't know. She's been acting like they were an item since Homecoming, but I don't think he was into her. Whoever knocked her up must not be as alpha as Cole, so she's hoping to rope him into mating her instead."

I don't ask what mating means. I can barely think above the noise in my head. Cole said those things about me. To people who matter in his life: his alpha, his parent.

Whether they were true or not, that's how he represented our relationship to them. That's the way he talks about me in front of his pack and probably his friends, too.

I flop face down diagonally on my bed. "God, I'm an idiot." I still can't seem to cry.

"No, you're not."

"Yes, I am. Even after we were together I let him pretend to still hate me at school. Not acknowledge me. Not protect me. When the whole school acts like I'm a leper. I must have zero self-respect." A few hot tears leak out now.

"No. I would've taken Cole Muchmore any way he wanted to give himself too. He's a God at our school. In our pack. He's the king of the alpha-holes. And something about that brooding bad boy makes you think he might be redeemable."

"But he's not." Bitterness makes the words sizzle against my teeth.

That's the truth of the matter. Cole Muchmore is not redeemable.

I misjudged him completely.

"Thanks for telling me," I say heavily. "I just want to be alone now."

Rayne lays a hand on my back. "I understand. Let me know if you need anything. Ice cream. A baseball bat. Whatever." She scoots off the bed.

I don't bother lifting my head.

I thought my accident and Catrina's death were the worst things that happened to me. And they were; that night definitely ranks worse than this.

But right now it feels like my chest is ripped open wide and everything I cared about is spilling in a puddle around me.

COLE

. . .

I GET a *fuck you* text from Bailey, confirming what I already knew: Rayne told her.

I don't dare go over to her house after the pack meeting because my dad's keeping his eye on me. He even stayed sober and heated up a frozen pizza for us all for dinner.

Like we're bonding now. Like I made him proud.

My stomach roils with what I've done.

I keep trying to tell myself I did the right thing to throw Alpha Green off Bailey's trail, and to appease my dad.

But it's a lie even I know reeks like shit.

I go up to my room after dinner and try texting again. Please let me explain. *Can I come over tonight?*

Try my window and I'll call the cops. I don't need your explanation. I already know what you're going to say.

I stare at the screen. Fuck. I'll have to try to explain by text. *Adriana lied and said I got her pregnant. I got alpha commanded into saying I'd been with you, not her. My dad went ballistic and Alpha Green started in about the no human rule, so I made it seem like I was just fucking with you. Bailey, you know that's not true. We hold each other's secrets, remember?*

She replies, *Yeah, I know. You threw me under the bus to save your ass. I get it. Humans and wolves don't mix— especially considering our parents. So we won't. End of story.*

The *end of story* hits me like the worst punch to the gut. Up until now, I clung to the hope that once I reassured her it wasn't true, we'd be good. She'd understand, just like she's been cool about keeping us on the DL.

My fingers shake as I hold my phone and stare at the screen. The panic that has been gnawing in the background since I saw Rayne comes out full force now.

Bailey, I want to mix. I'm sorry, I just don't know how. I fucked up. It was a shitty way of protecting you, but I swear that's what I was doing. I didn't want the alpha asking if you knew about us, and I didn't want my dad to come after you or your mom.

No answer comes through, which is worse than anything.

Can I please see you in person?

Still nothing.

I'm taking her at her word about calling the cops.

I put my fist through the wall beside my bed.

Fuck!

BAILEY

"ANY CLOSER, you're going to get slapped." I speak without turning from my locker, sensing Cole's presence behind me.

"Turn around," he murmurs. "I'll take the slap, Pink."

I whirl and give it to him to so hard I gasp at the sting of my palm. He doesn't move, just looks at me with mournful eyes.

Everyone in the hall stops moving. Stops breathing, even. All eyes are on us.

"You don't get to call me *Pink*," I tell him through tight lips. "You don't get to call me anything." Several lockers down I see Adriana and her cheerleader friends gathered, staring with wide eyes. Adriana wears a wicked smile. Like it's her birthday and this scene is her present. Like she won.

Bitch.

I slam my locker shut and turn on my heel.

Cole catches my wrist to pull me back but when he sees the outrage on my face, drops it and holds his palms out in surrender. He looks terrible. His hair is messed up, he has dark circles under his eyes and deep lines between his brows like he's been worrying.

"Hold up, Bails. I just want to talk." He speaks in a voice so low I can barely hear it.

I make a show of looking around. "You sure you can talk to me in public? You wouldn't want anyone here to know you actually care about me, right? Oh wait—you don't. It was all a game. What was the object again? To bring me to my knees? Newsflash, Muchmore: I'm still walking."

If Cole still needs to pretend he's the bully to me, I'll let him. He can keep his alpha-hole image intact. Far be it for me to prove he actually has a heart in that chiseled chest of his.

He swallows. "You know that wasn't true. Everything I said was bullshit. I *told* you that." His shoulders slump. I can't deny the misery etched in every line of his face. I won't let it soften me, though.

I was stupid to look past the alpha-hole persona before. But he won't get any passes from me again.

I push past the onlookers, willing myself not to let the hot tears filling my eyes spill. Of course at the end of the hall I have to pass Casey and her friends.

Casey semi-blocks my way.

I lift my chin and pass without looking her way. I'm shaking, but I'm not the confused little outsider I was when I first came to Wolf Ridge High. I know their secret now. I know it's not me, it's them.

And I know the real truth about Cole; he's not an asshole. Or at least he's capable of something else. But maybe that's his best-kept secret. Maybe I really do hold all his secrets.

In the library, I plop down and pull out my Chromebook, on which I've been assembling the newspaper. I have all the features, sports and entertainment articles. What I lack is any real news.

I think of Mr. Findle, my journalism teacher back in Golden. "A real story is about news that means something to the readers. It isn't news the politicians, or in our case, administration wants to feed the population. It's the story someone is trying to hide. Or the one they don't want to talk about. Sniff that news out, uncover the wounds, expose the flaws. That is real journalism."

I still remember the headlines: *Two GHS Students involved in Fatal Tragic Car Accident.* And then the next month: *GHS Student Suffers from PTSD Following Fatal Accident.* And the third: *Students Remember Catrina Goldberg Through Tile Art Project.*

I remember the way the students huddled over the

paper reading and re-reading the stories the moment the papers came out. The way they talked in hushed voices. Some even cried.

I wanted to kill our editor John Yager for wanting to write about it. For asking to interview me. I refused to talk to him at first. But somehow he convinced me that the story would be healing for everyone.

He was right. And John Yager won a state journalism award and a thousand dollar honorarium for "his sensitive coverage of the tragedy that affected the entire student body of GHS".

I hated being the subject of those stories. And yet telling the truth, having my and Catrina's story told did help on some level.

I stare at my blank screen.

There's a story to be told here, too.

A story that, again, would put me in the spotlight and cause me a lot of scrutiny and discomfort. A story that drags my tragic experience out into the open for others to explore. It's the most important news there is to tell at WRHS. The news that means something to every student. News that could protect future students from suffering the same experience I had.

And not telling that news—keeping the secret to protect my own privacy—is not only cowardly, it could cause harm.

I draw in a deep breath and exhale slowly.

So… how do I write this?

COLE

I POUND three of my dad's beers after practice. He's passed out on the couch already, his beer gut hanging under his t-shirt and above his gym shorts.

I take a fourth upstairs to my bedroom where I collapse on my back on my bed.

Maybe I'll drink myself to death along with my dad. Funny how I was working so hard to keep shit together, to keep food on the table, maintain a C average so I can play football, keep my dad from combusting.

Suddenly none of it matters.

School, football team, pack, family. I could give a fuck.

Meaningless.

All that effort I made to fit some role I prescribed for myself. Alpha-hole without a cause. Football star. Jerry's son. Casey's brother.

I didn't even do a good job at any of those roles, but they drove me. Kept me in a lane I didn't even like.

And now I don't give a shit about any of it.

All I feel is pain washing over my body. From my head to my feet.

Is this what Bailey feels?

Is that what I did to her?

Because if it is, I want to punch my own face.

I should punch my own face.

I try it and succeed in breaking my nose. Blood spurts out and runs down the back of my throat. I don't move from where I'm sprawled.

"Cole?" Casey knocks on my door and then pushes it open when I don't answer. "Why do I smell blood? *Fates.*" She looks at me with disgust. "Did you do that to yourself?"

"Get out."

She puts her hands on her hips and stares at me. "So what happened? Adriana's pregnant and claims it's yours?"

My hand closes so tightly around the bottle of beer, I crush it, gashing my palm with the glass.

"Cole." Casey rushes forward and starts pulling glass out of my hand and tossing it into the trash.

"Is it yours?" she asks quietly.

"Fuck, no! I haven't touched her in a year." I give Casey a death glare.

She ignores it and continues picking out the glass. "But the hum... Bailey doesn't believe you?"

I stare down at my mangled flesh, feeling nothing. "No. It came out that I've been with Bailey, not Adriana. And Dad was there. And Alpha Green. And I didn't want them to freak out so I said all this shit." I want to punch myself in the face again. I close my hand with the broken glass and squeeze, embedding the remaining pieces deeper into my palm.

"Knock it off!" Casey shoves my shoulder and pries my fingers back open. "What shit? What happened?"

"Stupid shit. Mean shit. That I was using her to get even. That my plan was to ruin her. What I used to think about doing to her before I fell—" I swallow. Fuck, it's true. "Before I fell in love," I choke.

"And then I walk out and fucking Rayne is there in the hallway and she heard everything."

Casey's eyes round. "Oh shit."

"Yeah. So Bailey's done with me. And I can't even fucking look at myself in the mirror because of what I did to her."

Shame engulfs me.

"I don't know what to do, Casey." I never admit weakness with my little sister. Never with anyone, except Bailey. But I need female advice right now. "Is this salvageable?"

Casey's gone pale. Whether it's caused by my patheticness or the horror of what I've done, I'm not sure. "I don't know, Cole."

Even Casey's disgusted by me.

"Basically, you picked your alcoholic abusive dad over the girl you love. Good choice."

I don't even have the energy to glare at her. I rub my hand over my face, smearing blood and bits of glass across my jaw.

"Stop it." She smacks my hand away. "*Do* you love her?"

My eyes suddenly sting. Memories of Bailey flash in my mind.

Her standing below my bedroom window, silently staring up at me.

The wonder on her face when she first saw the abandoned playground.

The way she cried for me in her car.

Her cinnamon and honey scent.

The trust she handed me when I didn't deserve it.

Her willingness to explore a sexual landscape neither of us had visited before.

I was stupid to think she was weak. Or nerdy. Or deserving of my scorn.

She's complex but clear. Broken but strong. So much more courageous than I'll ever be.

I wanted to break her, but in the end, she broke me.

And I am fucking *nothing* without her.

"Jesus, Cole." Casey sounds shaken by whatever she sees on my face. Fuck, maybe it's the moisture in my eyes. "Then you'd better figure out how to win her back."

I lean over and retch the three beers I chugged onto the floor.

Casey yelps and scoots back out of the line of fire. "Disgusting. You are disgusting. You need to decide. Do you want to rise above and win the girl back or use Dad as your role model and just throw in the towel on any kind of decent life? From where I'm standing it looks like you already chose option two, so yeah. Good luck with that."

I drop back on the bed and close my eyes, wishing I could just pass out and forget the pain in my chest.

The room spins. I haven't eaten since breakfast and football practice was grueling today. I guess that's why the beers didn't stay down. I should clean myself and the floor up. I should get out of this bed.

But I just can't seem to make myself move…

CHAPTER 16

ailey

I WASN'T GOING to go to the game. I guess I'm truly a masochist. Doesn't this whole relationship with Cole prove that?

No, I don't want to go there.

We had moments I wouldn't trade for anything. And I know the truth about Cole. Underneath the bully and bluster, the swagger and cocky arrogance, is a compassionate, honorable young man who does the right thing when push comes to shove. Who takes care of the people he loves, even if it means taking a beating and pretending not to date the girl he cares about.

And I do know he cares about me.

He didn't fake it. He wasn't using it or trying to break me. He just... isn't in a position to be my boyfriend.

And I forgive him everything. Because for all the pain of this breakup, he gave me so much more.

And that's why I'm sitting in the back row of the stadium with Rayne, watching him play football. I couldn't stay away.

I spot his dad down in the front, a beer can in his hand.

When the teams trot out, Cole's head is down. He gets in place for the first play and runs it with a decided lack of enthusiasm, losing the ball to the other team.

The spectators on our side grumble and mutter. I hear Cole's name spat out from all directions. I guess his fans are fair-weather only.

Which pisses me off.

I hope his friends aren't, too.

I sit and watch the disaster of the first half with a knot in my stomach, my hands balled on my lap. Cole's a mess. A total mess.

And it doesn't soothe my ego to know it's over me.

It just makes me die inside.

"You want anything?" Rayne asks as everyone rises from the benches to stretch and get food.

"No." I don't move. My body feels so damn heavy. My limbs weigh a million pounds. Rayne leaves and I sit and stare out over the crowd.

They're shifters. Probably most of them. Funny, but I don't feel like an outsider anymore. Wolf Ridge is my school. This team, my team.

None of that makes sense, but in finding out just how different I am, I finally fit in.

Maybe just knowing I share their secret.

That was what brought Cole and I close, too. The vulnerability of shared secrets.

I hardly notice when Rayne returns and the game starts back up. I'm numb from all the sorrow.

But then Cole comes out and I'm riveted to his figure again.

The whistle blows, the ball snaps. Cole catches it. Someone from the other team tackles him.

And then Cole goes apeshit nuts.

With a clear display of supernatural strength, he pushes up, flipping both their bodies so he lands on his back on top of the other guy, who is on his back on the ground. And then he turns around and starts punching the guy.

The referee blows the whistle non-stop. The crowd screams and boos—both teams alike. Cole's teammates jump in and drag him off the guy and his coach barrels out shouting.

"Rough play. Player number twenty-six is disqualified," the referee says over the mic.

I can't hear what the coach is screaming, but it's clear he's livid with Cole. Cole stalks to the sidelines but just before he gets there, he stops and tears off his helmet.

And looks straight up at me.

I don't breathe.

He doesn't move.

His coach is shouting at him. The crowd is booing. And then they start muttering. "What's he doing?" or "Who is he looking at?" The people around us twist in their seats, looking around until everyone in our section lands their gazes on me. Or at least, I feel their gazes on me. I'm not looking. All I see is Cole's anguished face, his burning gaze only for me.

I lift my fingers in a hesitant wave.

He lifts his chin.

Two of his buddies grab his arms and forcibly haul him off the field.

I bite my lips to keep from bursting into tears, even though I don't even know what I'd be crying for.

For Cole.

For me.

For us.

What can't be.

We sit through the rest of the game, although I see none of it. Honestly, I don't even know if Wolf Ridge won or lost. I probably would've sat there all night if Rayne hadn't grabbed my arm and hauled me to my feet to walk to my car.

Out in the parking lot, I hear the sound of raised female voices, but I ignore it. The cheerleaders are over by the ballers' cars where they usually hang out, ready for their post-game partying.

"Bailey!"

I look over at the group. Cheerleaders and a gaggle of other girls I vaguely recognize.

Rayne grabs my arm, like she's worried.

"Bailey!" It's Casey at the center of the throng. She's holding Adriana's upper arm in a bruising grip and drags her through the group of girls toward us.

"Tell her," Casey snarls, shaking Adriana. She's tall, bigger than Adriana even though she's two years younger. And she definitely shares Cole's gift of intimidation.

"Tell me what?" I ask. Chills run down my legs. What does this have to do with me? I really can't take any more of the Wolf Ridge drama.

Adriana bares her teeth in a distinctly wolf-like gesture and tosses her hair. "I'm not telling her anything."

"Fine, I'll tell her. Adriana's not pregnant. She never was. She made it up to cause trouble."

I fight to swallow, force my clammy hands to uncurl. Why does Casey think I'll care? Why does *she* even care? And the biggest why of all—why is she bringing this out in a public place when she knows her brother never claimed to have a relationship with me? That he denied and hid his relationship with me?

"It doesn't matter," I croak. "I don't care."

Casey's chest falls. She stares at me for a moment. "Well, I do." She spins Adriana around to face her. "You cause trouble for my brother or his girlfriend again and I will personally kick your ass." She releases Adriana with a push.

"Yeah," some of the volleyball girls agree.

Adriana's friends catch her. She pales. Casey definitely appears capable of fulfilling the threat.

"I'm not his girlfriend," I mutter, but no one hears me. The girls are starting to yell at each other again and Rayne tugs me away, eyes wide. "Someone's trying to fix what's broken," she says when we're at my car.

"Yeah, what do you think that's about?"

"I think she doesn't like seeing her brother go down so hard."

Goosebumps run down my arms. "Over me?" I whisper, even though I know that's the only answer.

"Um, yeah?" Rayne uses the *duh* tone of voice. "He just got kicked out of the game down there. He's definitely having a hard time with your breakup."

I shake my head and start my car. "You can't break up what never was."

"Oh don't give me that. You may not have had a label, but you two were definitely something. Something big and important to both of you."

Her words make me wince from pain. He was something big and important to me.

Is still.

I pull out into the line of game traffic. "Not important enough for him to go public with. Even his sister is more willing to admit we were a couple than he is."

Rayne rubs her forehead. "Right."

I wend my way through the packed streets until I get to our neighborhood where I drop Rayne off.

The lights are all off and there's no cars in the driveway at Cole's house when I get home, which is a relief. I don't need to wonder what he's doing. Whether he's thinking about me. If his chest hurts as badly as mine.

But I guess after tonight I know the answer.

He's hurting.

Wish that made me feel even one scrap better, but it doesn't.

~

COLE

. . .

IT'S 10:45 p.m. when I pull up in front of Rayne's house. Her mom will probably kill me for ringing the doorbell at this hour, but I don't give a shit. Coach Jamison pretty much kicked my ass after the game. He threw me up against the lockers and told me if I was going to act like a punk, I was off his team.

"I'm off, then," I hurled back at him, but he slammed me up again.

"Don't you dare quit on me, Muchmore," he growled. "Stop acting like a child who has no control over his life."

"I don't have control!" I yelled.

"Then take it," Jamison said quietly. "No one's in charge of you, but you, Cole. Not me. Not your dad. Not the alpha. Are you going to let them take your girlfriend away from you?"

I stared at him in shock. But of course he would know what's going on with me. My friends would've spilled when I almost ruined the game. They would do anything for me, but Jamison is alpha and like a father to all of us.

And that's when total calm settled over me. Calm and determination. "No," I vowed. "No, I'm not."

So I'm here. To figure out how to fix this mess I made. Finding out from Casey what Adriana did only makes me more determined. I march up the steps and ring.

Her mom, a production floor worker at the brewery, answers the door and squints at me, like she's trying to figure out what's going on. "Cole Muchmore?" she asks in disbelief.

"You've gotta be kidding me." Rayne's voice carries from wherever she was and she appears a moment later in the doorway.

Instead of inviting me in, she steps out on the porch and shuts the door in her mom's face.

"What do you want?" she demands, folding her arms over her chest. She's two feet shorter than I am, but apparently lost any fear she might have had for me in the past. Bailey did that for her. Gave her the confidence she'd been missing.

I shove my hands in my pockets to appear less threatening. "Advice. I need your advice. Or your help."

She raises a brow. "*You* need *my* help?" Her tone drips disbelief.

"How do I win Bailey back?"

Her mouth opens in surprise. Some of the hostility leaks away. But she says, "Don't you think you should just let sleeping wolves lie? I mean, you can't be with her anyway. It's forbidden."

I kick her front step. "I don't give a shit if it's forbidden. Garrett Green married a human," I say, referring to our alpha's own son. "A bunch of his pack members mated humans. Why is this pack so damn old-fashioned I can't even date one?"

Rayne shrugs. "I don't know. Are you willing to go up against the alpha on it?"

It's a test. I realize she wants to know how far I'd go for Bailey before she tells me anything.

"Yes," I say with total and complete clarity. "I'd go up against Green. My dad. My friends. Whatever it takes. I'm willing to fight for her. Is that what you want to know?"

Rayne shrugs. "That's what she needs to know."

I stare at her, trying to assimilate what she's telling me.

"You made her feel like she wasn't worth claiming

216

publicly. Like you were ashamed of being with her. If you want to fix this, you'd better show her you're proud to have her as your girlfriend."

My heart rate picks up speed. What she's saying makes sense. I humiliated Bailey by talking that way about her in front of my dad and the alpha. She may have understood I was lying, but she couldn't forgive the lack of respect and honor I showed her.

"Thanks, Rayne," I mumble. "That makes sense." I back down her sidewalk, my brain spinning on problem-solving. How do I prove myself to her? How do I show her I will always defend her—publicly and privately?

CHAPTER 17

 ole

IN WOLF CULTURE, the biggest and strongest always wins. It's survival of the fittest. Dominance and pack order. I don't know how long it's been since I've been bigger and stronger than my dad. It happened some time this past year.

I knew it before the neighbor Lon suggested it was time I fought back, but I wasn't willing. Before my dad became an alcoholic. Back when he was a good father, he taught me respect for my elders. Even now, when he's no longer worthy of my respect, it's hard for me to break that pattern.

But it has to be done.

My dad is toxic to this family. I'm not going to blame him for what happened between me and Bailey. That's on me. My bad choices. But I'm sure as hell not going to use him as an excuse to not have the one good thing that's shown up in my life.

And I'm not going to let him ruin my sister's future, either.

After practice, I walk through the house, picking up empty bottles and tossing them in the recycle bin. Some time in the last month, my dad switched from beer to Jack Daniels. There are four empty bottles in the kitchen. I find three partially full ones around the living room. I pour them down the drain.

"Hey!" my dad hollers from the living room, where he'd been snoozing in front of the TV. "What in the hell are you doing?"

"Getting rid of your liquor, Dad," I explain calmly.

Casey appears at the top of the stairs, a wary witness.

"Like hell you are. Put that down, Cole! Put it down, now!" My dad surges out of his chair and comes stumbling at me.

It takes all my concentration not to react in the usual pattern of fear or defensiveness or avoidance. I'm the alpha now. I can take him if I have to. "You're done drinking yourself to death. I'm not allowing liquor in this house," I say, like I'm the parent and he's the child. "And you're going to start AA meetings and clean the fuck up, or you're out."

My dad swings at me.

I duck and punch him in the gut, hard. Really fucking hard. The quicker this goes down, the better.

He doubles over and falls to his knees.

"This is my fucking house," my dad slurs, still

clutching his stomach on the floor. "You can't tell me what to do."

"Watch me." I channel Alpha Green. I put no anger in the words. Just the calm, firm confidence of a leader. "You have two kids in this house who need a stable environment. You're going to provide it for them. You're going to clean up and get a job. And if you don't, you'll be out on the street."

My dad lunges straight from the floor to my legs, tackling me to the ground. I kick one leg free then him in the face once. Twice. Three times.

Casey screams.

I kick him again.

"You're killing him, Cole!"

I kick one more time. He goes still.

"Fates," Casey breathes, dashing down the stairs and leaning over our dad.

"I'm the alpha of the house now," I tell Casey. "He can man up and be a dad or he's gone."

Casey bursts into tears.

I touch her shoulder and she steps into me, lets me hold her while she breaks down and weeps.

"It's over," I tell her. "We're going to be okay."

Bailey

I slept about three hours last night. My anxiety level is off the charts, but it's too late to back out now. The first edition of *Wolf Ridge High School Gazette* comes out today.

It's not the news article I wrote for the front page that has my stomach in knots, although that's the one that gave me nightmares last night. No, it's the first person account I wrote for the back page that made me chew my nails down this morning. I outed Cole in it. I stripped him of the power he holds—held—over me. I won't let him hide behind his bully persona anymore. He's a hero to me, and I'm going to reveal it to the whole school.

I'm letting the truth come out. That's what newspapers are for, right?

Rayne and I leave campus during lunch. I tell the gate monitor I'm on official newspaper business and he can call Brumgard to check it while I go pick up the newspapers at the print shop in Cave Hills.

"Do your school administrators know you're printing this story?" the sales clerk at the print shop asks me curiously.

Good. That means I wrote a powerful headline. *Wolf Ridge High Teacher Sexually Assaults Student* is the kind that makes everyone stop to read.

"They're about to find out," I say.

"Good for you," she says, helping us carry the boxes to my Beetle. "Way to hit him in the nuts."

"Thanks. I'm kind of freaking out, but I know it's the right thing to do."

"Definitely," the clerk says.

"It's going to be epic," Rayne says. "I am so proud to be your sidekick right now."

I grin at her and take a deep breath. "Ready to do this?"

"Ready."

"Let's go."

∼

COLE

WE COME in from lunch and I instantly sense the buzz. There's an energy in the air—a nervous, wired emission from every kid.

Newspapers.

They all have newspapers.

"Cole!" One of the JV ballers hands me one. It takes me half a second to read the headline and I understand.

I run for Brumgard's room. Bo, Wilde, Austin and Slade are at my heels. Asswipe's in there, eating his lunch at his desk. Probably hasn't seen the paper yet. I slam my palm against his door. "Guard this door," I order and Bo and Wilde instantly throw their backs up against it. Wolf shifters operate in a paramilitary structure. We're soldiers by nature, ready to give our lives for what matters, always following a chain of command. My friends haven't even read the article, but they respond with instant ferocity, trusting my war-like instinct to secure Brumgard's classroom.

Within thirty seconds, a crowd of underclassmen join them to stand guard.

"You two cover the window outside," I order Austin and Slade.

They nod and jog off, half a dozen volunteer recruits on their heels.

I scan the article quickly. It's a completely fact-based news article, written in the inverted pyramid style Brumgard taught us: most important news first.

WRHS Senior Bailey Sanchez was sexually assaulted by journalism teacher Alfred Brumgard on October 6th in his classroom after school. The assault, not yet reported to the authorities, was witnessed and interrupted by Senior Cole Muchmore, who reportedly stopped in to pick up extra credit work from Brumgard.

Muchmore physically assaulted Brumgard to stop the incident, resulting in the teacher's broken nose.

Sanchez, the victim, said, "I am bringing this story to the public now because I want to be sure it doesn't happen to anyone else."

Muchmore will reportedly testify as a witness in the case, if necessary.

Bailey Sanchez is a genius. A brave, brilliant genius. My eyes smart.

"Cole." One of the kids near me says. "Read this one." He flicks open the paper to another article. The headline is, WRHS *Student Shares First-Person Account of Assault.*

My heart starts pounding as I read it.

By Bailey Sanchez

This article is difficult to write, but I want my story to be known. I'm a new student at Wolf Ridge High. An outsider. I didn't have many friends when I started here, and I still don't.

When I asked my journalism teacher, Mr. Brumgard, if he'd be open to starting a student newspaper, he initially refused. But then, I believe because he saw I was friendless, he suspected I would be easy prey. He invited me to meet with him about it after school. Once we were alone, he offered his sympathy at my friendless state, pledged his friendship, and stuck his hand up my skirt.

At night, I lie in bed and think of the things I wish I'd done when it happened. What I could've done differently to prevent it in the first place, or how I could've defended myself better.

I'm ashamed to say that in the moment, all I did was freeze like a deer in the headlights.

But I'm lucky. Cole Muchmore, a WRHS football quarterback, walked in at that moment. We weren't friends. In fact, I would have said we were the opposite. But that didn't stop Cole from taking immediate action to protect me from my molester. The moment he saw my predicament, he slammed his fist into Mr. Brumgard's nose and told him never to touch me again.

When I ran away, he followed to make sure I was okay. He offered his assistance if I wanted to press charges.

Even though I understand the shame of sexual assault should belong to the perpetrator, not the victim, I didn't want to come forward. I didn't want my story known, or for people to think I'm broken or damaged.

But after much deliberation, I decided it was better to come forward and tell my story to prevent what happened to me from happening to another social outcast or otherwise vulnerable girl who comes to this school.

I don't want to be pitied. I don't want to be whispered about or pointed at. If you see me in the halls after you read this story, I'd prefer a fist-bump or high-five. Or just a simple, "Hi, Bailey," would be nice.

I smack my head against the lockers. How could I have ever been so cruel and insensitive to Bailey? Even after I, personally, had softened toward her, I never lifted my ban on the rest of the students forming friendships with her. They followed my lead, my orders. She's been walking around this school as an outcast since day one because of me.

I smack my head against the locker again.

I thought I was breaking her, but the truth was, she came broken. She came broken from her best friend's death, and then Brumgard broke her more.

But she put herself back together.

She rose above everything, above me and the shit I said about her, above Brumgard, above every student at this school who snubbed her. And she did it, not by putting up a front and pretending to be strong.

No, by showing her vulnerability.

Bailey Sanchez has more courage than anyone I know.

I smack my head a third time and a light hand touches my shoulder. "Mr. Muchmore?" It's Señora Cok, the Spanish teacher. "I think you'd better come with me to the principal's office."

To the office—right. Because Brumgard is going down. I walk with Señora Cok to the principal's office.

Bailey's standing outside the door and Principal Olsen opens it and beckons us both in.

I follow Bailey in. She's wearing one of those mini-dresses that drive me insane, this time with an old-fashioned rounded collar and knee-high socks underneath. She's unique and beautiful and definitely the coolest thing that ever happened to this campus.

But the metallic scent of fear tinges the room. She's nervous.

I walk straight over and take her hand, even though I have no idea if she'll let me hold it. "You have nothing to be afraid of," I say firmly.

Principal Olsen turns quickly around. "That's right, you don't." He holds up the paper. "I have one question for both of you." He points at the top article. "Is everything in here true?"

"Yes, sir," I answer.

Bailey nods.

Olsen picks up the phone. "Call in the sheriff. And get Coach Jamison over to Brumgard's classroom to make sure he doesn't try to leave."

"I already took care of that," I interrupt.

Olsen raises his brows at me, but nods, listening to whoever is on the other line. "That's right. Yes, let Green know, too."

He hangs up the phone and looks at Bailey. "I'm very sorry about what happened to you. Do you want to call your mom or should I?"

Bailey closes her eyes. "My mom," she groans. "I'll call her."

"All right. You two sit tight in here until the police

arrive. I'm going to check on the Brumgard situation. Cole, you say you took care of it?"

"I stationed ballers at his door and window. He's not going anywhere."

"Good work, Cole." He drops a hand on my shoulder. "You handled yourself well. I'm proud of you."

I want to roll my eyes, because that's what the old me would do, but for once an adult's praise feels honest and deserved. I accept it as the honor it is. "Thank you, sir."

He leaves the room.

"Bailey—"

"Let's not, Cole." She sounds tired. Strained. She pulls her hand away from mine.

I step closer but don't touch her. I have so much to say and this is the first chance I've had for a face to face alone.

"Bailey, I fucked up. I hurt you, and I'm sorry."

Pain ripples over her face and she looks away, out Principal Olsen's window.

I touch her cheek to bring her gaze back. Not insisting, just stroking softly. "Give me another chance, babygirl, and I'll do everything right this time. I will go toe-to-toe with Alpha Green and my dad and anyone else in the pack who thinks I shouldn't be with you. I will put a fucking crown on your head and parade you around this school as my rightful queen. If you give me another chance, I will be the best fucking boyfriend this town has ever seen—this world," I correct myself, spreading my hands wide.

A ghost of a smile appears on Bailey's face. "What does the best boyfriend do?"

I grin, because I can see her resolve crumbling. "I don't know, but I sure as hell am going to figure it out. I'm gonna watch my girlfriend and figure out what she needs from me, and give it to her."

Bailey ducks her head. When I nudge her chin back up, tears glitter in her eyes.

I want to grab her face and claim her mouth like I've done before, but I call on my restraint. "I need to kiss you, babygirl. May I please kiss you?"

She reaches for me. Pulls my face down to hers. Kisses my lips. She tastes sweet, like candy. I stroke my lips over hers, savoring the softness, the beauty of forgiveness.

Outside the office, I hear the deep voice of Alpha Green and I break off the kiss. "Come here, babygirl. I have to do something." I take her hand and lead her out of the office.

Green stands in the office, his imposing figure taking up all the energy in the room. He breaks off his conversation with the office manager when we come out. "Cole. Bailey." He nods in our direction.

Bailey jerks in surprise that he knows her name, but I squeeze her hand.

I clear my throat. "Bailey, this is, uh, Mayor Green, who is also our alpha."

Disapproval slams down on Green's face at my pack betrayal, but I stiffen my back. "Alpha Green, when we spoke at the meeting, I lied about Bailey. She *is* my girlfriend."

Green frowns at me. "That's forbidden, Cole."

"There's more. She knows about us." I swallow at the disapproval on his face. "She knows because she was cornered and bitten by a wolf last full moon."

"*Which. Wolf?*" Green demands, fury blazing in his eyes.

I hesitate. Ratting out others has never been my gig. But he bit my girlfriend. And I just promised to give her everything she needs. That includes justice. "Ben Thomasson."

"I see." Green surveys Bailey with an inscrutable expression. The office staff, all shifters, look on with avid interest.

"Bailey, I'm sorry for your experiences, both with Ben Thomasson and with the teacher at this school. I hope Cole has shown you a better part of Wolf Ridge."

She looks up at me, eyes soft and squeezes my hand. "Definitely."

"Does your mother know about us?"

She starts. "My mother. No. I was supposed to call her."

"Cole has sworn you to secrecy?"

"Yes, sir." I don't know how she knew to call him *sir*, but she's right on target.

Green picks up one of the newspapers. "There will never be an expose like this on the pack, will there?"

Bailey shakes her head. "Never, sir."

"Nor will you tell your mother or any other human."

"No, sir."

"Thank you, Bailey. We appreciate the contribution both you and your mother are to Wolf Ridge." To me, he says, "Cole, lies and breaking pack rules have consequences."

"Yes, sir," I say.

"I expect your complete honesty in all dealings."

I lift my chin to expose my throat and prove my submission. "I know, Sir."

"But I understand your home life has been difficult lately. Punishment already served. The pack has failed you and your sister. It's time we stepped in to do something about your father."

"I have it handled, Sir."

"You do?" Green raises his eyebrows. Bailey turns her big brown eyes on me.

"I do. I dropped him off to work at Circle K this morning. Jack Brown gave him a job."

Bailey squeezes my fingers, still searching my face.

Alpha Green nods. "I'm glad to hear it, Cole. I'm sorry if we failed you and your sister these past months."

"You did," I say, because I'm shooting straight now. "And apology accepted."

This wrests a grudging smile out of the alpha, but there's no time for more, because the sheriff arrives and Bailey and I have to give our statements.

We finish as the last bell rings. I sense Bailey's tension as we head out into the sea of students pushing through the halls.

"Hey." I tuck a protective arm around her and pull her against my side. "I got you, babygirl. From now on. Promise."

∽

BAILEY

. . .

WALKING through Wolf Ridge High with the homecoming king, star quarterback as my escort is a totally new experience.

The crowds part for us. People admire. Smile at me. Speak to me.

"Hi, Bailey."

"Hi, Bailey."

"Hey, Bailey."

"Way to go, Bailey." I get smiles, and waves and high-fives the whole way. Every single one of them rips down my walls even more. Today, I bared myself to the entire school.

And they received me.

I'm shaking by the time we reach my locker. Not out of fear. Just emotion.

Cole crowds behind me and wraps an arm around my waist, spreading his palm over my belly. "You're trembling, Pink," he murmurs. "Are you okay?"

I nod, a few tears leaking out. "It's nice to be acknowledged," I say, turning around to face him. "I guess that's what happens when I'm escorted around by the king of the alpha-holes."

He shakes his head. "No. That was all you. It was the article you wrote. You won their respect, no thanks to me." He pulls me into his chest and wraps me up tight, pressing his lips to my hair. "Pretty soon, I'm going to be introduced as the journalist's boyfriend."

"Ha." I laugh into his chest. It feels so good to touch him again. To feel his strength and solidity. To breathe in his scent and know he's got my back. I bite his pectoral muscle through his shirt.

"Hey." He laughs and pulls back. "I must be rubbing off on you. Are you trying to mark me?"

"I have no idea what that means, but it sounds fun."

His eyes flash yellow for a moment and he crowds me back against the lockers. "Careful what you wish for, little human," he rumbles in my ear right before he attacks me with his mouth.

EPILOGUE

*C**ole*

FRESHLY SHOWERED AND CHANGED, pumped with post-game endorphins, the alpha-holes jog out of the locker room and push through the throng toward the parking lots.

We just trounced Cave Hills. They're our biggest rival, not because they're great ballers—at least not football. Rich humans' parents don't let them play the sport because of the concussion thing. No, the rivalry is more due to proximity and the economic disparity between our two communities.

Bo scans the crowd in the direction of the guest team parking lot.

"Who are you looking for? Gone in Sixty Seconds?"

"Shut up. Don't call her that."

"Is she here?" I start scanning, too, wanting to see the human who has Bo's balls all twisted.

A moment later, he goes rigid. I follow his line of sight toward a tall, leggy human who stands a head above the other kids around her. She's stunning just in sheer size, but also gorgeous, with long, caramel-colored hair.

"Catch you guys later," Bo mutters, veering off.

"Sure you will," I call back.

My own balls tighten in anticipation of finding Bailey in the crowd.

I find her standing by her car with Rayne, but the two aren't alone. A group of girls is gathered around them talking and laughing. Over the last couple of weeks, Bailey's been integrating more and more into the Wolf Ridge social structure. That means Rayne is, too, because Bailey isn't the type to abandon a friend when her social status changes.

"Pinkalicious," I call out as I approach and then run in to grab her waist and toss her up onto one shoulder.

She giggles, her thighs squeezing my chest and back as she rocks on her perch three feet above everyone else. "Show off."

I bite her inner thigh and she creams her panties. The scent makes me growl. I fucking love handling her like a doll, showing her how much more powerful I am than she is. Giving her a reason to swoon over me.

I've been working my ass off to prove I'm worthy boyfriend material. I publicly stake my claim on her every chance I get: picking her up, carrying her, holding her hand, pulling her into my lap at lunch. She goes soft for all of it. Looks at me with those warm brown eyes and makes me feel like a hero.

There was one fight with my dad over it. A short one

that involved me showing wolf eyes and fang and telling him he'd better goddamn respect her or we're done and he backed down. It's a work in progress. He's been sober for two weeks, going to AA meetings every night and working at the convenience store every day. He's depressed and defeated, but at least he's not drunk.

He's a smart, capable man. At least he used to be. He'll figure his shit out.

"What's up, Rayne-bow?" I fist-bump the runt, who was trying to fade into the background. "You hanging with us tonight?"

"Sure." She shrugs like slumming with our group is normal and she didn't just shoot from outcast sophomore to hanging with senior royalty.

"Put me down, Cole." Bailey's squirming. Riding my shoulder's getting her too horny for her own comfort.

I swing her around and drop her down to straddle my waist, my forearm under her ass. She twines her arms around my neck and kisses me. I want to drag her out of here alone. Take her up to Austin's cabin and fuck her blind.

But she's enjoying the social thing. And I deprived her of it for way too long to deny her even one night of partying and fun.

I pop Bailey to the side, to ride my hip like a mom holds a toddler. "What's the plan, Austin? You're our social director, right?"

Austin shrugs. "Mesa?"

Same plan as ever, only now it's different. Now I see it through Bailey's eyes and it's all fresh and new. All tinged with excitement and sexual electricity. I bite

Bailey's neck. "Can't wait to get with you," I murmur in her ear.

She shifts restlessly on my hip, grinding her clit against me.

I carry her over to the side of my truck and push her ass against it, shifting her to straddle my waist again. I shove the bulge of my cock into the cradle of her legs. "Austin said the cabin's ours tonight. Unless Bo shows up with his hot car thief and we have to fight him for it."

"You'd win," she purrs. "But there's more than one bedroom."

"I know, Pink, but as much as I love holding you down and covering your mouth when we fuck, I also want to hear you scream." I ease my hips back and then thrust again. "And tonight you're going to be screaming my name until you're hoarse."

Her smile stretches a million miles. "Promise?"

I groan because I don't know how I'm going to wait until I get her alone. "Wolf's honor."

WANT to read what happened when Cole sneaked through Bailey's bedroom window? There is a bonus scene available only to my newsletter subscribers. If you're not already a member, sign up here: http://sub-scribepage.com/alphastemp

Thank you for reading my first "bully romance." I hope you loved it. If you did, I would so appreciate your review and recommendations. They make such a difference for indie authors.

. . .

—SIGN **up** **for** **my** **mailing** **list**: http://subscribepage.com/alphastemp

--**Get text alerts of my new releases** by Texting: EZLXP55001 to 474747

--**Join Renee's Romper Room**, my Facebook reader group by emailing me with the email you use for Facebook. It's a secret group (because we discuss kink) so I have to send you an invite to join.

ACKNOWLEDGMENTS

I'm so incredibly grateful to Lee Savino and Aubrey Cara, who both dived into this book and helped me make it so much better. Also to Mary and Hayley for their beta reads.

Thank you to the members of Renee's Romper Room for your support and love (if you're not a member and you're on Facebook, please join!). Thanks to our ARC readers and to Ardent Prose PR and the bloggers who support my releases. You are all amazing!

WANT MORE?

Check out Alpha Knight, Book 2 in the Wolf Ridge High Series

loane

STEALING the 2016 Porsche 911 is the easy part. At least it's the fun part. This is only my second car theft, but I think I have a real gift for it.

I'm dressed as daddy's spoiled princess in a pair of Rag & Bone skinny jeans with wedge heels and a Balmain cropped tee. All remnants of my past life, when I really was daddy's spoiled princess. When stealing a car meant lifting a pair of keys out of my dad's lock box and choosing one of the twelve sports cars in his garage.

My hair is pulled up in a twist, and I have a khaki rhinestone ball cap pulled over my eyes to hide my face.

Anyone who glances over in this crowded parking lot will see someone who matches the car.

It's just a matter of finding the right make and model in a location without camera surveillance. I've been walking around the Scottsdale mall parking lot for days now, dodging cameras and mall cops.

Finally, I spot one. A blue Porsche 911 Carrera 4 GTS, and it looks to be full leather interior. *MSRP* can range from 100k to 200k depending on the engine and gadgets inside. I know because my father had one just like it sitting in our garage before... before the fall. Before everything went to shit. Before I had to learn how to poach pretty cars out of mall parking lots.

In theory, ordinary cars are best—the kind that blend in. But I don't have the luxury of time or lower risk. I'm on a payment schedule with dangerous people, and the Porsche will bring in big bucks.

So the Porsche it is. I already bought a totalled version at the salvage yard, so I have a salvage title. Now all I have to do is swap some parts out, including the VIN, and retitle this baby to sell.

Unfortunately, that means trusting a chop shop to do the swapping and cutting them in on half the proceeds because I don't have the skills.

Yet.

I plan to learn. In fact, I think I'll see if the guy can teach me on this one, so the next car I can do on my own.

I walk up to the car like I own the place. Like I own the Porsche, I mean.

Like I own the house and job or father or husband that

match this car. It's a role I know intimately. Lived my whole life. Entitled. Cosseted. Spoiled.

Daddy's little girl has fallen far from grace.

My device does its work, and the locks pop. Another few seconds and the car revs, and then I'm driving wild and free.

Out of the parking lot. Onto the highway.

Up to Wolf Ridge, the weird-ass community just past Cave Hills.

Right where I landed when my dad went to jail.

Bo

I RIDE my 1984 Triumph to the shop after football practice because we've been slammed, and my brother and uncle need me around more than just on the weekends.

Plus, my best friend Cole's been no-showing for work lately. I don't know what the fuck his problem is, but I'm not gonna bust his balls considering the shit he's been dealing with at home this semester.

I'm starving, which makes me cranky as hell.

But I forget all about the hunger because... *hot damn.*

The first thing I see is her ass. Fuck-hot-amazing ass in tight jeans that show every curve of her muscular cheeks. And looooong fucking legs punctated by platform heels that lift everything.

I give a silent hooty-hoo whistle in my head in appreciation.

She's leaning over the engine of an electric blue 2016 Porsche. My brother Winslow is beside her, pointing something out.

At first, I assume she's a shifter, like most everyone in Wolf Ridge and try to figure out who she can be.

Then I catch her scent.

Human.

Human who should've been a shifter. Because she's built like a she-wolf. Tall. Big-boned. Sturdy, athletic. She didn't get those lean muscular legs lying around on her bed playing on her phone.

No, she works for them.

And—holy hell—when she lifts her torso and turns, my dick gets hard. Because she's young. Maybe my age. And beautiful. Caramel-colored hair with reddish highlights, copper eyes that match, and a beauty mark that makes her look like an old-fashioned movie star.

I want to fuck her right up against that 911. Then I see the logo stretching across the front of her tits. *Cave Hills Cross Country.*

That explains the legs. And the expensive car. Looks like someone wrecked Daddy's ride and brought it up here to get it fixed before he finds out.

Maybe because I'm hangry or maybe because she got my dick hard and I know I can't have her, but I take an instant dislike to her. Fucking Cave Hills spoiled little rich bitch. Cave Hills kids only come to Wolf Ridge when they're looking for trouble. And this girl is definitely trouble.

Winslow catches sight of me. He stops what he's saying to level me a *what-the-fuck-do-you-want?* look.

And that's when I know something's off.

Because he wouldn't use that expression because I interrupted him with this chick. He wouldn't be hot for a human girl—Winslow hates humans.

Which means he wants me to stay away for some other reason.

"Don't you have a door to replace on that VW?" he jerks his thumb toward the other bay. We were waiting for the new part to be delivered, and the VW was his project, not mine. Now I'm certain he's trying to get rid of me.

"Yeah. Okay." I still don't move.

Prickles raise on the back of my neck. I look at the Porsche again. Maybe it's not her daddy's ride. What were they looking at under the hood?

Unease washes over me. It's a familiar warning—the kind I get every time my big brother is about to do something really stupid. Or dangerous. Something I'm gonna have to try to talk him out of or stop.

Fuck.

Please tell me it's not a stolen vehicle, and he's about to help this girl fence it.

When I don't move, Winslow's lip curls, and his eyes flash yellow. The wolf in me experiences the threat viscerally.

I have no choice but to drop my gaze and lift my chin, showing my throat. My brother has a mean streak, and he's dangerous as hell, even though we're family. I toss my backpack down and head to the bay with the VW Beetle in it.

Winslow turns the radio up on his side.

. . .

ALPHA KNIGHT

WANT FREE RENEE ROSE BOOKS?

<u>Go to http://subscribepage.com/alphastemp</u> to sign up for Renee Rose's newsletter and receive free books. In addition to the free stories, you will also get special pricing, exclusive previews and news of new releases.

OTHER TITLES BY RENEE ROSE

Paranormal

Wolf Ridge High Series

Alpha Bully

Alpha Knight

Step Alpha

Alpha King

Bad Boy Alphas Series

Alpha's Temptation

Alpha's Danger

Alpha's Prize

Alpha's Challenge

Alpha's Obsession

Alpha's Desire

Alpha's War

Alpha's Mission

Alpha's Bane

Alpha's Secret

Alpha's Prey

Alpha's Sun

Master Me Series

Her Royal Master

Her Russian Master

Her Marine Master

Yes, Doctor

Double Doms Series

Theirs to Punish

Theirs to Protect

Holiday Feel-Good

Scoring with Santa

Saved

Other Contemporary

Black Light: Valentine Roulette

Black Light: Roulette Redux

Black Light: Celebrity Roulette

Black Light: Roulette War

Black Light: Roulette Rematch

Punishing Portia (written as Darling Adams)

The Professor's Girl

Safe in his Arms

Sci-Fi

Zandian Masters Series

His Human Slave

His Human Prisoner

Training His Human

His Human Rebel

His Human Vessel

His Mate and Master

Zandian Pet

Their Zandian Mate

His Human Possession

Zandian Brides

Night of the Zandians

Bought by the Zandians

Mastered by the Zandians

Zandian Lights

Kept by the Zandian

Claimed by the Zandian

Stolen by the Zandian

Other Sci-Fi

The Hand of Vengeance

Her Alien Masters

ABOUT RENEE ROSE

USA TODAY BESTSELLING AUTHOR RENEE ROSE loves a dominant, dirty-talking alpha hero! She's sold over a million copies of steamy romance with varying levels of kink. Her books have been featured in USA Today's *Happily Ever After* and *Popsugar*. Named Eroticon USA's Next Top Erotic Author in 2013, she has also won *Spunky and Sassy's* Favorite Sci-Fi and Anthology author, *The Romance Reviews* Best Historical Romance, and *Spanking Romance Reviews'* Best Sci-fi, Paranormal, Historical, Erotic, Ageplay and favorite couple and author. She's hit the *USA Today* list five times with various anthologies.

Please follow her on:
  Bookbub | Goodreads | Instagram | Tiktok

Renee loves to connect with readers!
www.reneeroseromance.com
reneeroseauthor@gmail.com

Click here to sign up for Renee Rose's newsletter and receive a free copy of *Theirs to Protect, Owned by the Marine, Theirs to Punish, The Alpha's Punishment,*

Disobedience at the Dressmaker's and *Her Billionaire Boss*. In addition to the free stories, you will also get special pricing, exclusive previews and news of new releases.

Made in the USA
Monee, IL
20 January 2024

51529534R00157